About the author

Andy Clancy is a former police officer, now working as a security contractor in the UK and overseas. He lives in Hastings. For more information on Andy Clancy and his novels, visit his website at andyclancy.co.uk.

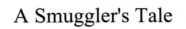

A Smuggler's Tale

Andy Clancy

A Smuggler's Tale

Vanguard Press

VANGUARD PAPERBACK

© Copyright 2018
Andy Clancy

The right of Andy Clancy to be identified as author of
this work has been asserted by him in accordance with the
Copyright, Designs and Patents Act 1988.

A CIP catalogue record for this title is
available from the British Library.

ISBN 978 1 784653 54 5

*Vanguard Press is an imprint of
Pegasus Elliot MacKenzie Publishers Ltd.*
www.pegasuspublishers.com

First Published in 2018

**Vanguard Press
Sheraton House Castle Park
Cambridge England**
Printed & Bound in Great Britain

This novel is dedicated to those I know and love, who now walk with the angels.

'No business carried on in Hastings was more popular and extensive as that of smuggling. Defrauding the revenue, so far from being considered a crime, was looked upon as a laudable pursuit, and the most successful "runners" were heroes. Nearly the whole of the inhabitants, old and young and of every station in life, were, to some extent, engaged in it.'

John Banks, Hastings schoolteacher, 1871

Prologue
Waterloo 17th June 1815

What was left of the soldiers of the 2nd Battalion, 35th Sussex Regiment of Foot were formed into their own square. Six hundred or so men gathered together to survive. To the outside, several lines deep, were the privates, corporals and sergeants, their once familiar red jackets covered with the filth of a day in battle. Nervous eyes appeared through faces blackened with the smoke of cannon and musket fire. The square was three lines of soldiers on each side. The front rank kneeling with the butts of their muskets pushed firmly into the ground and their barrels with 18 inch triangular steel socket bayonets fixed; pointing outwards making a barrier that horses instinctively shied away from. To the inside were the rest of the regiment, cooks, quartermasters, drummer boys, officers and the colonel of the regiment. It was the first time in the whole day that the soldiers of the Sussex Regiment had felt in any way safe. They knew they had formed a square to defend against cavalry attack; they had been savaged all day by Napoleon's artillery, at least defending against cavalry gave them some respite from the carnage of cannon balls that had decimated their regiment. As they waited for the attack to come, the square formation of the regiment resembled a field bristling with hedgerows of bayonets on four sides.

It wasn't just the Sussex Regiment, the whole allied army was ready for the cavalry attack, what was left of the mixed force of English, Dutch and troops from Brunswick, Nassau and Hanover were in the same formations; as long as they kept their discipline they could withstand the French cavalry attack and stop them penetrating the squares. If they wavered, the result would not just be defeat but complete annihilation of the whole army.

To form an army of thirty thousand men into different squares was no easy task; officers rode around on their horses making sure the army was in a checkerboard formation to prevent one square firing a volley of lead musket balls into another.

To the front of the reformed allied army were the artillery, they were under orders to fire at the French cavalry on their approach and then run back in to the safety of the squares. The officers and men of each gun crew were nervously looking ahead; all they wanted to do was fire their guns and run back, each man looking at which square was the closest one they could run back to.

Sitting astride his horse, surrounded by staff officers, was one man; overseeing from afar the manoeuvres, which would decide the fate of the battle, was the commander of the allied army, the Duke of Wellington. How calm and in control he looked; what was he thinking inside?

Captain Hamish Munro and Sergeant Major Daniel Sibson were amongst the veterans of the Sussex Regiment; together they commanded one complete quarter of the square. Walking up and down the lines of soldiers, both men were doing their best to keep the men's spirits up. The men were exhausted; they had been in constant battle for almost five hours, they were starving hungry and dying from thirst so that their lips almost stuck together because their mouths were so dry. Seeing this, Captain Munro lost his temper and shouted at a drummer to run back to the centre of the square and get the quartermasters to bring water for the men.

Looking Daniel straight in the eye, Captain Munro told him, 'Sergeant Major, the men are flagging! Get them up for this fight! You know what to do; this attack is the one we have to stop!'

Daniel didn't need to be told twice. 'Now, lads, I know you can do this; you've faced them how many times before. Remember Spain: you kept their damn cavalry out then, you can do it today. Keep your discipline.'

Daniel knew all his men, the inexperienced and the veterans; he slapped the young ones on the back and nodded and winked in a knowing way to the men who had served with him all the way from the war in the Spanish Peninsular to this moment.

'Who's your best friend, lads?' Daniel shouted.

'Brown Bess!' came back the reply in a loud chorus of shouts.

This was Daniel's moment to really gee the men up, 'that she is lads, knap those flints, get your cartridges ready and let's show these Frenchies how the Sussex Regiment can fight!'

There was a massive cheer in response; the men took off their Belgique Shako helmets waving them in the air along with their Brown Bess muskets; they were ready.

Corporal Ralph Masters was one of the veterans. 'We're a long way from Hastings, Daniel; I wish we were there in the fishing village now. Will we get through this?'

Daniel looked hard at his friend; they had grown up together in the fishing town of Hastings on England's south coast, joined the army together and fought the armies of Napoleon all the way through Spain, surviving the many battles and engagements. Daniel cared for all his men, but, if there was one man he wanted to stay living, it was Ralph.

'Believe me, Ralph, there's no place I'd rather be now than back in England, but I promise you I'll get you back home. I got you through Spain, didn't I?' Daniel smiled as he said it.

'That you did, Daniel. I know we'll be drinking ale together back in the town when this is over.'

Those were the last civilized words that either man would speak; their heads were turned away from each other by a thundering noise that sent shivers down their spines.

There was a rumbling, quiet at first and then it got louder, until Daniel and Ralph thought all the hounds of hell were coming at them. Then they appeared through the mist and smoke of gunpowder from a day of battle, squadrons of them in the most disciplined formation. French cavalry, cuirassiers, hussars, lancers, dragoons; Napoleon must have released all his cavalry at once, thousands of them, charging at the allied force, the bruised and battered allied force that had withstood Napoleon's attacks all day.

It was a truly magnificent sight, this was Napoleon's gamble, he had softened up the allied army with his relentless artillery bombardments and Infantry attacks, now he would sweep them from the field with his cavalry.

Closer and closer the squadrons of cavalry came until every horse was being ridden at full charge. The British artillery outside the squares waited for the order to fire their cannons.

Inside the square, Captain Munro's men gratefully drank the water that the drummers and stretcher bearers poured into their field cups.

Satisfied his men had something to drink, Captain Munro turned back to Daniel. 'Right, Sergeant Major, that's better. Have the men prepare their muskets, ready to fire.'

As the order went out, soldiers on each side of the square were doing the same thing. Years of practice made the drill of loading a musket a natural action. Almost without thinking, each soldier pulled a cartridge from the black leather box resting on his right hip. The top of the cartridge was bitten off and held in the soldier's mouth while gun powder from the other half of the cartridge was poured down the barrel of the Brown Bess. The musket ball was then spat into the barrel, no time for ramrods this day, and the butt of each Brown Bess was tapped on the ground to make sure the musket ball went to the bottom of the barrel. The musket was lifted up and the remaining powder from the cartridge was poured onto the musket flashpan that was then covered over with the frizzen to stop the priming charge from pouring away. With that done, in less than a minute, six hundred muskets were loaded, primed and ready to fire.

The French cavalry were less than a hundred yards from the line of artillery. No man inside the squares could hear the order, they just saw and heard the guns fire; the result was devastating for that first line of cavalry. A mix of cannon balls and grapeshot tore through the once ordered squadrons. Men and horses, the ordnance didn't discriminate; it destroyed everything it hit. As men were thrown from horses they buckled forwards, the impetus of the charge was effectively broken as the squadrons had to pull up momentarily behind the chaos of their dead and wounded comrades. This was the opportunity the gunners were waiting for: they ran for their lives before they were ridden down by the French cavalry. Clambering to get back inside the squares, the gunners collapsed on the ground, breathless and relieved that they had escaped the French cavalry sabres and lances.

Recovering from the artillery volley, the hordes of cavalry regained their momentum and swarmed around the different squares. It was now the turn of the infantry to face the full force of the charge. Captain Munro nodded at Daniel.

'Make ready your muskets!' Daniel shouted above the din of battle.

Each soldier put his musket into the port position.

'Present!'

The second and third lines of the square went into the aim position, with fingers on triggers and the hammers of their muskets cocked backwards, ready to fire.

As the French cavalry came at full pelt to his side of the square Captain Munro knew what he was doing, he wanted the cavalry within fifty yards of his men where their Brown Bess' were most effective.

Each soldier was transfixed, staring at the mass of men on horses coming straight at them, in their hearts praying to hear the order to fire. Captain Munro nodded at Daniel.

'Fire!' Daniel screamed at the top of his voice.

A whole line of muskets spat out flames and lead musket balls at once. At almost point blank range, the impact was devastating, French cavalrymen flew backwards, sideways, forwards in every direction off their horses. Stallions whinnied at being hit by musket balls and tumbled forward, throwing their riders in front of them. The charge was again stopped in its tracks; it became a melee of horses and soldiers trying to barge and trample their way forward over dead and wounded men and animals.

As the next line of cavalry approached, the order came out around the whole square: 'Independent fire at will!'

The square, as well as being a jagged steel formation, was now a constant firing operation as each redcoat fired without waiting for further orders.

Bugles sounded and the different cavalry squadrons turned and retreated. As they rode away, the soldiers of the Sussex Regiment waved their Shakos in the air cheering.

'Well done, lads! Now load up, ready for the next charge,' ordered Daniel.

Again, the French cavalry charged and at each charge they were repulsed, the gunners ran back out to their guns, fired a volley and ran back into the squares, with this and the musketry and discipline of the allied squares, the French casualties were appalling.

During a pause between charges, Captain Munro asked Daniel, 'Are you thinking the same as me, Sergeant Major?'

'Yes, sir, I am. Cavalry attacking with no infantry support, no artillery barrages between charges... either it's yet to come or they got it wrong this day.'

'I pray to God you are right, Sergeant Major. We can keep their cavalry off for sure; look, here they come again,' said Captain Munro, turning his attention to the next charge.

For some reason, Daniel was counting the charges in his head, but after the seventh he stopped counting. The French cavalry had lost all order and organisation and were riding around each square desperately trying to find a way to break into them. Some were firing their cavalry pistols, others were riding as close as possible to the rows of pointed bayonets leaning over their mounts trying to bash the barrier of steel aside with their sabres, but try as they might, they couldn't pierce the square.

Captain Munro and Daniel were everywhere, encouraging the men, standing them up, patting them on the shoulders and calling stretcher bearers for the wounded.

Captain Munro noticed, in the melee, that his men were dropping down after being hit by musket fire. 'Where? Who?' he thought to himself, peering through the ranks of redcoats, smoke and charging horses and then he saw them: French Dragoons, sitting back on their mounts, firing into his men with their cavalry fusils, reloading and firing again.

'Sergeant Major! Over here, now!' he shouted.

Daniel sped over to him and, after a brief conversation, ran back to the ranks, speaking with a dozen of his experienced men – all good shots from the Light Company – before he got to Ralph.

'Still alive, Ralph?' asked Daniel.

'I am indeed, Daniel,' answered Ralph, lifting his Brown Bess after shooting a Hussar off his mount. Amidst all the slaughter they had a moment to smile as the French cavalry still swirled around the Sussex Regiment square.

'Good shot! Captain Munro has orders for you; you see those dragoons sitting still on their mounts, firing? You are to fire at them, and any Frenchman you see with a musket or pistol in his hand, and nothing else until they get the message. Have you got it?'

'I have, Daniel, yes.'

Patting Ralph on the shoulder and winking at him, Daniel ran off back down the line to lead his men.

Ralph and the other veterans from the Light Company went about their work straight away. A French dragoon loading his fusil was lifted back off his horse as a musket ball hit him square on the chest; another dropped his musket as he was hit on the leg, falling off his mount in agony.

Ralph bided his time until he saw his target, a French dragoon officer riding around his men organising them.

'Au revoir, monsieur,' he mouthed to himself as he pulled the trigger on his Brown Bess; the musket ball hit the officer square on the side of his helmet, killing him instantly.

It wasn't long before the dragoons knew what was happening; the men of the Light Company were finding their targets and they were dying. The dragoons rode off into the midst of the hundreds of other cavalrymen, Captain Munro's tactic had worked; it was almost impossible to load a musket while riding a horse.

The men in the Sussex Regiment knew they were winning, they kept their discipline and the square stayed as one. Dead horses and French cavalry lay in heaps around the squares – surely they would give up soon?

Bugles were sounded, horses started to turn and ride off – this was it, they had broken them!

Standing together with Daniel, Ralph took his Shako off and leaned on his musket. 'Well, Daniel, we're still here.'

Before he could answer, their heads turned as they heard shouts and more musket fire. A French cuirassier had turned back from his retreating comrades and charged straight at the square, ducking down on his mount he avoided the musket balls that flew past him and just as it looked as if he would charge straight onto the row of bayonets he pulled back on his reins.

The cuirassier made an almighty jump into the square, straight over the heads of Ralph and Daniel. Ralph crouched down, he stood up turning, as he did so the cavalry giant was behind him, he swung his sabre and caught Ralph across the left arm before he could lift his musket, the sabre cleaved his arm straight through above the forearm, Ralph was in shock as he watched part of his arm fall away with the hand still gripping the barrel end of the Brown Bess, he froze looking at the armoured giant sitting on the charger. Time stood still for Ralph as the cuirassier lifted his sabre again, this time for the killing blow.

'Bang!'

The cuirassier's right eye exploded in a bloody mess as a musket ball went through it and out the back of his helmet. He dropped to his left and fell off the horse; Daniel had made the killing shot.

Somehow, Ralph was still standing as blood poured from the stump of his severed arm. He looked at Daniel and fell forward into his arms.

'Get a surgeon here, now!' Daniel screamed, he had stopped being a Sergeant Major and became a lifelong friend again.

'Stay with me, Ralph; I'll have you back in Hastings, I promise you.' He looked into his friend's face while holding his hand over the bloody stump that was once Ralph's arm.

'I know you will, Daniel,' he smiled and then sank into unconsciousness.

Captain Munro had seen the whole incident from afar; he walked over to where Ralph lay attended by his friend. There was nothing he could do, on this terrible day he had to care for all his men, but he knew the friendship of the two men he stood over.

'Sergeant Major, stay with Corporal Masters for now.'

Daniel looked up and murmured, 'Thank you,' as Captain Munro walked away.

Several hours later, the battle was over. What was left of the French army was completely routed; they weren't in retreat, they were a disorganised mob on the run. As for Napoleon, who knew or cared where he was!

Daniel sat on the ground surveying the day's carnage all around him. He had fought many battles in his army life but this was the worst, he had never seen so many dead and wounded men on one field. Ralph was lying on a stretcher on the ground; he was drifting in and out of consciousness. Ralph's stump of an arm was bound up, somehow the surgeon had stopped the bleeding. Captain Munro, as was his way, went about the exhausted men of the Sussex Regiment talking to them and doing his best for the wounded, he too was tired and sank down on the ground beside Daniel.

'I think we fought our last battle, Sergeant Major,' he thought out aloud.

'You're not wrong, sir. After this day, I never want to see another battlefield for the rest of my life.'

The men's voices stirred Ralph back to consciousness. Ralph was weak, but he noticed Daniel beside him and lifted his remaining hand up. Daniel held it.

'That's it for us, Ralph, no more fighting Boney; we're going home to England.'

'It'll be better there, won't it, Daniel? The people back home will remember we saved them from the French, won't they?' He was almost pleading.

'Of course they will, Ralph; it'll be a fine life for us back home.'

'Was it worth it, Daniel? All this slaughter, all this misery?' Ralph thought he was dying and was after reassurance.

'Of course it was, Ralph. We saved England from Boney. We'll get our jobs back at the fishing village, we'll be fine, just you wait and see.'

Captain Munro stood up. He seemed uncomfortable as though he couldn't bear to listen to the conversation. Daniel, looking at him caught his face; Captain Munro said nothing but his silence and facial expression were deafening. As he walked away Daniel's words of comfort resounded in his mind but he found no solace in them. Thinking about all the good men he had commanded throughout the war and on this terrible day at Waterloo. He knew better about what would happen to them when they got back home to England.

Chapter One
The Welcome Home – Hastings, South Coast of England 1817

The old shop in Hastings town hadn't changed a bit. It was full of everything from pots and pans to clothing, sugar and lumps of salted meat hanging on hooks from the ceiling. It was a warm and comfortable place, with an open fire that gave some respite from the biting winds and cold of the English Channel that blew into the town from just a few hundred yards away. The merchant viewed the collection of medals that were on the counter; picking them up, he looked at some closer than the others and smiled to himself.

Placing the medals, almost respectfully, back on the counter, he pushed them back towards the two disheveled men standing in front of him. 'I would like to help you both but I have no interest in buying these from you, I'm sorry gentlemen but these medals are something you should keep.'

They were used to being rebuffed; it had become part of their daily life since their regiment was disbanded after returning home from the continent. Doors were slammed in their faces, people ignored them, walking past as if they were dangerous felons out to do them harm. But this man was different in his manner, he was almost apologetic.

Daniel gathered up the medals and was about to put them back into the tattered canvas bag where he kept his few meagre belongings when the merchant's hand touched his arm. Daniel looked back at the merchant as poor one-armed Ralph curiously waited to see what the man behind the counter wanted.

'Let me show you something my friend,' he lifted up his jacket and shirt to reveal a large jagged scar under his rib cage.

Daniel and Ralph looked at each then back at the merchant in a manner of recognition.

'You served as well?' Ralph asked.

'Aye, I did just like the both of you in the Spanish peninsular, fourteen years in the 1st Regiment of Foot Guards, I loved it and hated every day in equal measure!'

He laughed loud and long after he said it, so did Daniel and Ralph, they knew what he meant.

'I got this beauty from one of Napoleon's damn Polish lancers at Talavera, lucky for me he couldn't get the lance tip full in or I wouldn't be here now.' He pulled his clothing back down and leaned under the counter to grab an object that he placed on the counter, it was a service medal identical to those belonging to Daniel and Ralph. It had clasps on it representing the same battles the two men had fought in, Corunna, Talavera, Badajoz, Vittoria, and Salamanca to name a few.

'My name is Bill Crisp, sit you down for a moment and let me do my best to advise you some.' Gesturing to two old wooden stools, he proffered his hand and both men gladly shook it.

As the two men sat Crisp hung a kettle on a wire over the open fire to boil some water, he looked at Ralph. 'Well, I told you about my scar. How did you lose the arm?'

Ralph was startled; he was used to people turning away when they saw what was left of his left arm, not asking about it. He was almost pleased to tell his own story.

'Waterloo, a cuirassier managed to get into our square, he chopped this bit off before I knew what he was about, Daniel here plugged him before he finished me off!' He looked at Daniel and smiled who turned away shyly, he had his own reasons.

Crisp, sensing a somber moment, chipped in, 'Cuirassiers with those heavy breastplates; do you remember how they would roll around like turned over turtles on their backs when we knocked them off their horses? How they would struggle trying to get up, even in the middle of battle? It made me laugh!'

Crisp had an ability to cheer things up and so the three Napoleonic veterans laughed again with a sense of humour only they would understand.

Any form of kindness had been a rare experience since their return to England; Daniel and Ralph sat and cupped their hands around the warm mugs of tea that Crisp had made them. As they talked, they felt friendliness and a welcome they hadn't experienced in a long time. Crisp was straight-talking with both men and it was obvious he himself had gone through everything they had lived in the past eighteen months.

It wasn't just Daniel and Ralph; they were everywhere. Men in tattered redcoats of their regiments they had worn since they were fighting in the Spanish Peninsular, America and Belgium. They all looked the same, gaunt, thin, or walking with a limp or a missing limb. Yes, they had saved the nation from "Old Boney" but that was it now, no one wanted to know them. The veterans were an embarrassment because the country knew they had bled for Britain and now Britain had turned its back on them: no reward, no thanks, nothing. The fact was, people were tired of the war, they didn't want to know about it and they certainly didn't want to be reminded about it by the men who fought and won that war. The lucky veterans had families to support them and, in fairness, many an officer from the different regiments tried hard to find work for their men but this was piecemeal. Every village, town and city had them, Napoleonic veterans, thousands of them and not a job to go between them; a fishing town like Hastings on the south coast was no exception.

'I made my decision to leave the army when Boney was exiled to Elba; I bought this place with the money and everything I plundered in my years in Spain. Maybe I was wise, perhaps I was lucky, but here I am and here you are both without a penny to rub between you.' Crisp drained the last drop of tea from his mug.

'Well Bill, you're not wrong about the money, we have no family left here, nothing. We thought we'd come home to a hero's welcome, we couldn't have been more wrong. We used to be fishermen, but there's no work for us here any more and I've lost count of how many places we've been kicked out of on our backsides.' Daniel smiled at Ralph as he said so.

'I told you both I didn't want your medals as I have my own from Talavera and the rest. As for your Waterloo medals, you know yourself they are two-a-penny these days; maybe one day they'll be worth a lot, wouldn't that be a thing? Besides, even if you sell them, you might live off the money for a week, then what will you do?'

'We're listening, Bill.' Both men were expectant, waiting to see what was coming.

'You both learned many things in the army, you have abilities that are of no use to most people but there are those who may find you very useful, even those of you with just the one arm.' Bill smiled at Ralph.

Before Daniel could speak Ralph, put his arm across him.' We've been gone from this town over ten years, Bill. Cut to the quick and tell us what you're about, you know how desperate we are.'

'Aye, it's obvious you've been away from Hastings for a long time; much has changed here. If I mentioned smuggling, what would you say?'

'Smuggling? Well, when we were youngsters here, the odd ship would come in with a bit of tea that'd be taken off at night to avoid the duty being paid, we all knew about it,' Daniel answered.

'Well, it's no longer the odd ship, as you say, with a bit of tea. While we were off fighting the French, people in the town here got organised. Aside from the fishing, smuggling is what keeps this town living: gin, coffee, sugar, spices, jewelry, silk, gold... Anything you can think of is brought over from the continent now, so there's money to be made from it if you know how. Well, there it is, you can carry on begging, selling your medals or get involved, what's it to be?' Bill stared hard at each man.

'You already know our answer, tell us where to be and what to do Bill,' Daniel answered.

At that, a woman walked into the shop and Bill turned his attention to her. 'Wait there, gentlemen, we have more talking to do.'

As they waited impatiently for Bill to deal with the woman, for the first time in they didn't know how long, Daniel and Ralph felt that they had something to look forward to. They were both anxious for the woman to be about her business and leave them to continue their conversation with their new friend.

Bill dealt with his customer politely and after she purchased two small hard paper bags of sugar and salt she left the shop. Turning back to the two veterans he asked, 'So, gentlemen, where were we?'

'You were saying, Bill, about making money out of smuggling if you knew how,' Daniel replied enthusiastically.

'Yes, so I was. Let me speak frankly; ships come in from time to time and men are needed to unload them. We call them "tubmen"; you carry things off the ship in barrels over your shoulders or have them tied around your front by a rope – you don't even need two arms to do it!' He smiled and winked at Ralph, at this the three men laughed again.

Bill continued. 'You do the work and you empty the contraband off the ships, that's it. I give you fair warning from the off, the smugglers here are quite ruthless, you watch your mouth around them, if they think you are talking to the duty men, the town constable or whoever they won't hesitate to slit your throat. Just do as you're told and you get ten shillings for a night's work, how do you find that?'

'What do you think, Daniel?' Ralph turned to his friend.

'What I think is that we have nothing! We followed Wellington across all of Portugal and Spain for how many years and you lost your arm at Waterloo. Now here we are, selling our medals to buy food, so here's what I think. Remember all the men we buried in the Peninsular and Belgium, who remembers them? I'll tell you: no one. So what do they care about us? Nothing. So now we do what we do to survive... yes, if it means we join the smuggling gang to survive, so be it!' He looked back at Bill, his mind made up.

'Good, come back here tomorrow, here's some coins to keep you going in the meantime, but don't waste it on grog, do you hear me?' Bill fished into the pocket of his waistcoat and took several silver coins out, handing them to Daniel. Both men's eyes opened wide at this.

As Daniel put the money in to the pocket of his tattered coat Ralph seemed troubled, 'Bill, you are being very kind to us and I thank you but what's in it for you, getting us into this?'

Daniel became nervous because of Ralph's question, fearing he would dash their first piece of good fortune in a long time.

Before he could chip in, Bill answered, 'Well, Ralph, it's quite simple: the whole town is involved in this enterprise.' He lifted his eyes as he said this. 'A man can be a fisherman in the day and at night he carries a tub full of contraband gin from the beach up onto the West Hill behind us. As for me, look around you – where do you think I get most of my stock from? It certainly isn't from Lewes or London. You could also say I'm on good terms with the man who runs things here his name is Dobson. I find him trustworthy, useful people like you to work for him and he, of course, shows his gratitude to me. So, if you still have any doubts, enjoy the new money in your pocket and forget we ever met. If you're still good for this, be back here tomorrow, like I said, so we can talk again.'

'Have no concerns, Bill. We're grateful and we'll back again to talk tomorrow. Our thanks for the money and your hospitality; I promise we will pay you back. Come on, Ralph, we're off now.' Daniel gestured to his friend. He wanted them out the door as he was scared that Bill would be annoyed by any more of Ralph's questions.

They shook hands with Bill and left, once outside Daniel turned on Ralph.

'You may be my best friend but there are times when I want to bash your head against a wall, what are trying to do asking stupid questions when we have a chance to earn money and decent money at that?' Daniel was furious.

'You know, Daniel, my mother used to say to me that if something is too good to be true, it usually is, that's all.' Ralph was as ever calm.

'My God, enough of your rhymes, what are you on about, Ralph? What are we doing wrong?' Daniel was becoming more frustrated.

'I know how desperate we are for money, Daniel, and sure we can earn ten shillings a night carrying contraband, but, mark my words, this will end badly for us. The army was hard, but at least we were doing the right thing for the king and our country. I'm with you always, Daniel, you know that, but this is wrong.'

Ralph turned and walked on, as Daniel followed behind his friend through the town he looked at the tall brown wooden huts where the fishermen stored their day's catch of fish and the stone cottages and buildings that sat upon the winding streets and alleys of his home town. He was back where he was brought up and he wanted to stay and if carrying contraband would let him then so be it. There were still doubts in his mind, Ralph's words had nagged him and he knew why, Ralph was right, one way or another, this would end badly.

It was a fine morning on the East Sussex coast as a lone horseman trotted on the main road from Bexhill and approached the beach at West St Leonards. As he pulled his mount to a halt, it gave him and his horse a chance to recover after a brisk early morning ride. While patting his horse on the neck the rider surveyed the lone Martello Tower at the seafront of West St Leonards. Over the previous fifteen years, Martello Towers had become a familiar sight on the south east coast of England, built to guard against invasion by Napoleon and his "Grande Armée". Each tower could hold over twenty soldiers, had an artillery piece aimed towards the sea and a number of slits where the soldiers could fire their muskets out of. Much to the relief of all of England, they were never tested against the French. The Martello Tower at West St Leonards was long since empty of soldiers as there was no threat from Napoleon any more. Instead, it was occupied by twenty men, a sergeant and a captain in charge of "His Majesty's Preventative Service", more commonly known by locals, smugglers and even themselves as "Duty Men". Their job was to prevent and detect smuggling wherever and whenever it occurred.

As Sir John Rutherford spurred his mount forward towards the tower he felt relief that once and for all there was no more war with Napoleon, he had seen it first-hand serving as an officer on the staff of the Duke of Wellington in the Spanish Peninsular and in Belgium. Sir John was proud to have served his country but any thought of the war brought back the sights of butchery he had witnessed and been part of and he quickly tried to rid his mind of the images but didn't always succeed. If Sir John needed a medicine for the troubles of his mind then it was all around him. Hastings, Bexhill, Battle, he was born and bred into the area as part of the landed gentry and he loved it with every fibre of his body and soul. The sea, the beaches, the cliffs, the rolling green fields, for Sir John this part of East Sussex was God's country and, as the newly appointed Magistrate for the area, he would do everything in his power to make it a good, safe place to live for all. It was this fondness for Hastings that brought Sir John to West St Leonards this morning, for there was a growing menace that had been allowed to fester unhindered during the war and up to the present time and it was now affecting the whole area and every person who lived in it.

This made him feel anxious and, at the same time, he was nervous for a different reason, dismounting from his steed he walked up to the battered wooden door of the tower, he was meeting the captain in charge of the Preventative Service and knew beforehand that he would not receive a warm welcome.

Ten minutes later, the atmosphere was tense as Sir John sat at a wooden desk looking across at Captain Hardwicke of the Preventative Service. A sergeant placed two mugs of tea down on the desk and exited the room quickly; he looked like another experienced veteran who knew what was coming.

Sir John began, 'Captain Hardwicke, my thanks for meeting me this morning. Let me get straight to the point of my visit. I am very concerned by the activity of the smuggling gangs working out of the area around the east and west hills of Hastings. In recent months, they have become brazen in their actions, smuggling is no longer their only line of work. They have begun threatening and extorting money from local people and businesses. Many decent, honest, hardworking people who live from day to day trying to survive are terrified of them. At this rate, I fear that unless significant action is taken against them, Hastings will become a town of lawlessness inhabited by criminals.' As Sir John spoke he became increasingly irritated by the behaviour of Captain Hardwicke who appeared to be taking no notice of anything Sir John was saying.

It was plain to see that Hardwicke wanted the meeting finished as soon as possible, he flicked through a pile of papers on the desk pretending to read them and not lifting his head as Sir John spoke. Hardwicke was relatively new in the post and was not a native of Hastings, neither was he a Napoleonic veteran and, as much as he didn't want to admit it, these points peeved him, especially when he talked to the likes of Sir John. As he turned another sheet of paper over, a hand slammed down hard on the pile of papers, flinging them everywhere.

Hardwicke sat back, startled, his face flushed red; he was now panicked, not disinterested. 'How dare you – who do you think are?'

Sir John leaned forward. 'Good, now I have your attention and you will do me the good grace of listening to what I have to say, you ask who I am, let me repeat myself as you obviously weren't listening before. I am Sir John Rutherford, the resident magistrate for Hastings, Bexhill, Battle and Rye and I need you to work with me if we are to deal with the smuggling trade that is blighting this area.'

Hardwicke now angry, had changed from being disinterested to resentful. 'Oh yes, you and everyone in this dump-hole town keeps telling me how organised and dangerous the smugglers are. I'm fed up to the teeth hearing this! Why are you all so scared of a few common criminals? I have already met with the Town Constable, Tappin; he has given me the names of the individuals involved and I will soon have them behind bars.'

The name of the town constable agitated Sir John further. 'Tappin? Are you serious, Captain? That man is completely in the pocket of the smugglers, I assure you that any information he gives you will be for the good of the very people you are trying to arrest not the Preventative Service.'

Before Hardwicke could reply, Sir John raised his hand, realising that a shouting match would achieve nothing. He took a breath and tried to calm the conversation. 'Captain Hardwicke, I apologise that I have caused you to be angry but let me assure you that what you have just said is true, they are organised and they are dangerous and you and your twenty Duty Men will not be able to deal with them on your own.'

Hardwicke paused for a moment composing himself, then delivered a speech he had been rehearsing in his mind for some time, prepared for yet another Hastings local telling him how to do his job.

'Tell me, Sir John, if you and how many others in the town know so much about this smuggling problem, why have you done nothing about it? Perhaps you lack the will or the knowhow? Well, these common criminals do not scare me nor my men and I have my own plans for dealing with your smuggling problem so here is my position, join with me, follow me or get out of my damn way!'

Sir John suppressing his anger stood up and leaned over the desk, 'I advise you strongly against any form of action until we are ready, in particular, do not speak with that idiot of a town constable, Tappin, of any operation you or we intend to take, he cannot be trusted.'

Hardwicke felt more confident after his diatribe. 'Why do you veterans of fighting Napoleon think you know everything? What's the matter, do you still want some glory?' He was goading Sir John.

'You would appear to have some knowledge of my service in the war, Captain Hardwicke. However, what I did in the army has nothing to do with our current situation but as you choose to bring it up, then I will mention one thing. If your enemy has clear knowledge of your intentions; then any battle is already lost before it is even fought, you would do well to remember that Captain Hardwicke. I would also remind you that smuggling is a practice that locals have been doing here for over fifty years. Do you really think you'll stop it in a few weeks?'

'I think we have talked long enough, Sir John. You are the magistrate for Hastings and you administer the law; I am the appointed captain of His Majesty's Preventative Service and as such I will enforce the law. Is there anything else?' Hardwicke started to shuffle the scattered papers on his desk back together.

Sir John was not done. 'Captain Hardwicke, I ask you to respect my opinion, aside from the war I have spent my whole life in Hastings, what was a few local smugglers has grown into a monster, you may arrest a few smugglers but that will not make the problem go away. I will be writing to the Home Secretary to meet with him in London for us to obtain the help we need.'

'London? The Home Secretary? My God man, don't embarrass yourself, I doubt the government has even heard of this place. You may write to the king if you wish, but may I remind you that I too have my superiors in London I can speak to if I see fit, which, at the moment, I do not! By all means, go to London if you wish; it will not change the course of action I intend to take.'

Sir John continued, 'I beg you, Captain Hardwicke, to give me time; I will get us the help we need to deal with these criminals for the long term.'

'I am confident I have enough good men to get the job done. As for help, it is not necessary. I bid you good day. Sergeant!' he called out.

As the sergeant escorted Sir John out of the tower, both exchanged a knowing look.

'You served in the army?' Sir John asked.

'Yes, sir, my name is Tinsley. I served with the artillery in Spain, Portugal, everywhere and now I'm a sergeant in the Preventative Service, so there it is.'

'Well, Sergeant Tinsley, your captain won't listen to me but this is my advice to you, follow that man and you may find yourself a dead sergeant in the Preventative Service. Good day to you!'

Tinsley said nothing in reply, he understood completely what Sir John meant and watched the magistrate as he strode away from the Martello Tower back to his horse.

Mounting his horse, Sir John rode away. He shook his head in frustration. 'This is madness, utter madness, I pray God nothing happens between now and my visit to London,' he thought to himself.

The Customs House in Hastings town should have been the home of the Preventative Service but Captain Hardwicke, for his own reasons, preferred to use the Martello Tower at the far end of the sea-front as a barracks for his men. The Customs House was a running joke in Hastings, purely because everyone knew that anyone working there would be in the pay of Dobson and his gang of smugglers. In fairness to Captain Hardwicke, he suspected this and wanted to keep his men as far from the town as possible so they couldn't be bribed. However, this was another reason why the trade went on unhindered.

Instead, the building was used by the Town Constable, a born and bred Hastings local called Tappin. The building was basic and in poor condition with a couple of rooms, one acting as an office, the other a makeshift kitchen and sleeping quarter. Tappin enjoyed being the town constable, there was no hard work involved and he made money, more money than he ever made in all the years he spent as a local fisherman. As for keeping the peace, Tappin was old, overweight and unhealthy. Besides, he had a number of watchmen working for him and patrolling the streets of Hastings with their lanterns at night, which was their job. The truth was neither the town constable nor his watchmen were the law in Hastings; that was controlled by the very people who kept Tappin and his men with pockets full of coin. The morning had begun as normal as any morning in the Custom House for Tappin, comfortably ensconced in the front office at his desk, he sat down to eat a breakfast of bread, cheese and hot beans out of a wooden bowl. Tappin had a habit of eating greedily, he slurped the food down in a hurry, bits of bread and cheese pasted around his mouth, he didn't care it tasted much too good. As Tappin stuffed his face, the main door burst open and two men walked in, one was a similar age to Tappin, short and stocky with a scarred, grizzled face but dressed in the expensive garb of a country gentleman, standing behind him the other man was young, tall and fit, not as smart in his dress as the older man but his very demeanour was intimidating. Tappin stood up surprised, knocking the bowl of beans over the desk, more food splattered on his face and shirt.

The older man laughed. 'My God, Tappin, you're not only fat and stupid, but disgusting as well! Where did you learn to eat, in a pig pen?' He laughed again, the younger man with him showed no emotion.

'I'm sorry, Mister Dobson, you surprised me, I wasn't expecting to see you this morning,' Tappin answered, trying to wipe his face with the back of his hand.

Dobson walked round the desk and stood directly in front of Tappin; the idea was to bully the town constable further and it was working. 'Why would you be surprised, Tappin? I pay you enough money so I reckon I can see you whenever I want. As it happens, I don't want to be anywhere near you cos you disgust me, but you have your uses, so stop feeding your face, close your mouth and open your ears. I need you to do something to earn all the silver I line your pockets with, tell me are you and the new captain of the Duty Men on good terms?'

Shrinking back from Dobson; Tappin was all ears. 'Yes, Mister Dobson, it's a Captain Hardwicke. What can I help you with?'

'Captain Hardwicke, you say?' Dobson place his hands on Tappin's shoulders easing him back down onto his chair, knowing he had him exactly where he wanted him, he then walked back around the front of the desk. 'Here's the thing, Tappin; I've heard talk that this Captain Hardwicke is ambitious, thinks he can teach me and my boys a lesson, is that so?'

'Yes, Mister Dobson, I have heard such talk.' Tappin was eager to please.

'Good, then in a few days you will go and see this Captain Hardwicke and you will tell him you have information of where and when a shipment of contraband will be coming into Hastings.'

Sensing an opportunity, Tappin dared to ask a question, 'Why would you want me to do that, Mister Dobson?'

'Let's say I want to teach this new Duty Man a small lesson.'

Tappin looked scared again when he heard this.

'Don't you worry, Tappin, I just intend to clip his wings a bit. One of my men will come and see you on the day it will happen; that's when you deliver the message to the Duty Men. Mark my words, though, if you mess this up, my man Harrison here will come back and use your face to practice on before his next bout, am I clear?' Dobson become menacing again as he patted the tall man on his muscled shoulders.

As quickly as he finished speaking, Dobson and his minder, Harrison, walked out the door and back into the street. Tappin slumped forward onto the desk, head in his hands, he was still scared and shaking and spoke aloud, asking himself, 'Why did I involve myself in this, why?'

A week after their meeting with Bill Crisp, Daniel and Ralph stood on the beach at Hastings under the cliffs of the West Hill, it was late and it was dark. The West Hill was historically significant for Hastings, it was on this hill in 1066 that William the Conqueror made camp with his invading Norman army. As Daniel turned to look at the cliffs behind him he felt a mixture of emotions, the scenery was magnificent and scary at the same time as the waves crashed onto the beach. It was a full moon and on nights like these, as Daniel looked at the cliffs, he thought to himself that there was no place more beautiful on the earth than Hastings and its permanent friend, the sea; he loved them both in equal measure. They were among perhaps forty men, all standing in a group. Bill hadn't told them much except to be there, say nothing, nod their heads and do what they were told and as two former soldiers this was something they could easily do. After a while, four men approached the group, the obvious leader addressed them.

'Right, listen up, for those of you who don't know me my name is Dobson and I run things here. So these are the men in my crew, Smith, he is my enforcer, he gets things done for me, Watson here, he keeps people happy, the town constable, the watchmen, he gets me what I need to know so no one bothers us. Harrison, my best fighter, look at the shoulders on him,' he said as clapped him on the back. 'One day, I'll have him fighting the likes of Cribb and Molyneaux; we'll have our own "champeen" of England and the world, mark my words. This is the deal, I pay you well, I pay you very well in fact, ten shillings for this night's work, but you do as I say. No questions asked, no discussion, whatever I say, you do it, all you do is say yes, if no, walk away and keep your mouth shut or I'll see to it you end up in the channel in bits to feed the gulls. So there it is. Questions?'

'What about the Duty Men, Mister Dobson?' a voice called out.

Dobson and the three men with him laughed. 'Don't worry about them, they're tucked up nice and warm in their Martello Tower at West St Leonards. Besides, we have people looking out for them. Enough of that now. Has anyone here served in the army?'

Daniel and several other men raised their arms, Ralph instinctively went to raise his one arm but Daniel held it down and smiled at his old friend.

'Good, you men go with my man Smith. The rest of you will work as "tubmen" and you go with Watson here to grab your straps and whatever you need, you'll be doing the donkey work tonight.'

Daniel and Ralph nodded to each other and went their separate ways.

Before they led their groups away, Dobson pulled Smith, Watson and Harrison together. 'So this is the night; Tappin has been down to the Martello Tower already. We can expect company tonight and, when they come, we'll teach them a lesson they'll never forget.' They then went their separate ways.

Smith brought Daniel and the other veterans to join with a dozen other men, all of them were obvious thugs by their appearance and demeanour. Daniel noticed a pile of muskets and cartridge boxes lying in a pile on the shingle beach.

Smith picked up muskets threw them to each man, 'Here, you should know how to use one of these.'

As Daniel looked at his musket and cartridge box he smiled to himself, it was a Charleville, a French military weapon, even the cartridge box was French they were obvious contraband items. How many of these had fired at him over the years! Veterans of the war were useful to Dobson, they had skills he could use and the fact was no one else would employ them, who else would know how to use a French musket?

'So listen up, you have your weapons, load them and fan across the beach and keep an eye out for any Duty Men, once the stuff is taken off the ships, we follow the carts up to the hill and we do the same thing up there.'

Taking up position on the beach with his cartridge box slung over his shoulder and musket in hand, Daniel felt comfortable, doing what he knew best.

The tubmen were standing in a group and the enforcers were watching out for the duty men. They waited for a long time, then there was activity, movement. Daniel looked beyond the beach to the sea, then he saw it: a light.

The light got bigger, then more lights appeared behind it, within a few minutes several rowing boats pulled up on the beach. Each boat was laden full of crates, boxes, barrels and, as the men on board spoke, it was obvious their mother tongue was French. The atmosphere was indescribable, exciting and the age-old smuggling operation that was tried and tested went into full swing. The men on the boats did their best to hold their vessels on the waves as the water broke on the beach. From everywhere, men ran towards the boats until barrels, boxes, crates were being unloaded, the tubmen were busy and standing at the back directing the whole operation was Dobson, old, grizzled, scars on his face from how many fights over the years and hard as nails. Dobson enjoyed the whole thrill of the operation, he was in his element. The operation went on for several hours as the boats left the beach and returned again fully loaded with more crates and barrels. As the boats were emptied, Dobson and Watson spoke French with several men who had come in from the sea, they exchanged handshakes and Dobson handed them bags that were large and heavy.

Daniel watched the whole scene, in between acting as a lookout, and couldn't help but be impressed. He was used to manoeuvres and operations in the army, but this was flawless; every man on that beach knew his job. Horses and carts with drivers were waiting, the barrels were loaded onto them, once done the drivers jumped on them and off they went up the track from the beach towards the West Hill.

The atmosphere in Hastings town was anything but excited, the taverns were empty, people stayed inside their homes, this was a night when you kept yourself to yourself, see no evil, hear no evil was the norm if you didn't want a problem. It was always the same when a ship was arriving with contraband. It was a poorly kept secret and how could it be kept secret when so many local people were involved in it.

Tappin was hiding in the Custom House, consoling himself with a tankard of beer; he had done what Dobson had ordered him to do and been to see Hardwicke. He hoped – no, he prayed – that Hardwicke would do nothing and stay away this night. In any case, Dobson had told him not to worry, holding this thought he filled his tankard with more beer and downed it in one go, drinking himself to oblivion he was sure to wake up in the morning and find that all would be well.

Back on the beach, the last of the rowing boats had emptied their loads and went back to their ship. Dobson and his gangers, satisfied the last of the carts had been loaded, gave the order and the train of carts wove their way up the track to the West Hill. Daniel and the other enforcers followed behind joined by the tubmen and the other hangers-on. Before long, the carts arrived at the top of the West Hill where there was a flurry of activity taking place with carts, which had previously arrived, being unloaded. It was then that Daniel saw the entrance to the caves. He hadn't seen or thought about them in years, he played in them as a child but they were different now. The caves were a warren of tunnels and spaces dug out over the years and the whole town knew they existed but paid little attention to them. Hundreds of years before people had once lived in them but their purpose had changed. Dobson had found his use for the caves; they were now a supply depot. Crates, barrels and boxes stored everywhere and anywhere. This was Watson's job; he was in charge and would have everything in order, clothes, silks, tobacco, alcohol, whatever the contraband was. Watson knew what was in each crate and barrel, how they should be moved and where they were to be stored. Looking around, Smith was nowhere to be seen;

slinging his musket over his shoulder Daniel followed his curiosity and the tubmen as they carried the barrels and crates through the entrance inside. The caves were a mystery to everyone except the smugglers, they worked in them, stored in them, slept and ate in them, it was their kingdom and no one but the smugglers would go inside the caves, not least the Duty Men. Daniel had never imagined they could look like this, he walked down a long passage into a large cavern that was illuminated by torches, this wasn't a cave it was a giant storeroom, with men loading their crates into piles organised by Watson.

'What do you think, Daniel?' It was Ralph with a small barrel under his good arm.

'What I think, Ralph, is what the hell happened to these caves? I've never seen the like before.'

'I know, Daniel. Still, a couple more hours and we should be ten shillings better off each. You were right; let's not think about it and take the money. You just be careful out there.' Ralph winked and went about his work.

Hearing the voice of Smith shouting, Daniel unshouldered his musket and ran back outside to where the other enforcers were.

Captain Hardwicke was in a confident mood, this would be the night when he and his men would put the smugglers behind bars, he didn't need help from London he thought to himself. The same could not be said for Sergeant Tinsley and the nine other Duty Men as they gathered in Hastings town waiting for orders to go up the West Hill. Sergeant Tinsley had seen enough battles but the men under his command were nervous, he knew none of them had ever seen a musket shot fired in anger, he looked at the faces of each man as they fidgeted nervously with their muskets and equipment awaiting orders to move.

Hardwicke addressed his Duty Men. 'So, which of you men knows a short route to get up the hill rather than following the path?'

Not a hand was raised nor was there an answer, the men including Sergeant Tinsley knew nothing about the West Hill. Hardwicke could feel himself becoming frustrated, more so as he knew he had listened to Tappin and reacted on impulse by deploying half of his whole command to the West Hill without corroborating the information the town constable had given him.

'Where is that Town Constable, Tappin, the stupid fat idiot? Probably locked away in the Custom House getting drunk,' he exclaimed aloud, but he was of course right in his assumption. 'So be it, we go up the path. Sergeant Tinsley, form the men up and follow me.' Hardwicke then started the long walk from the town up to the West Hill.

As the Duty Men followed Hardwicke, one of the younger men in the group called Stark turned to Sergeant Tinsley, 'So, Sergeant, what do you think?'

'What do I think? I think this is a fool's errand and it will end in tears. Whatever happens, stick close by me and keep your head down. Have you got that, lad?'

Stark nodded his head, so nervous he squeezed his musket and continued walking up the path. They were doomed men from the start, all of them. Dobson had spotters in the town who had watched them arrive in their horse-drawn wagons, form up and start their ascent of the hill, even before the Duty

Men had started up the path a horseman had already ridden up the hill to let Dobson know who was approaching.

Daniel and the other enforcers had been instructed by Smith to form a line facing the footpath that came from the town up the hill. As they waited, looking down the hill they could hear the sound of a horse coming at them at speed, one man raised his musket but Smith put his hand on the barrel and lowered it, 'Leave him be, boys, he's one of ours.'

As the horse and rider approached them, it stopped, both exhausted and panting from the uphill journey. Smith ran to the rider, they exchanged words and the rider rode off behind them to the caves. Within a short while, Dobson arrived and spoke with Smith then waving his arms gathered his men around him.

'So lads, it appears we might be getting visitors tonight in the form of Duty Men, they're walking up the hill now, are you up for a fight?' Dobson asked smiling.

Heads nodded all around him except for one, Daniel.

'Mister Dobson, I know these types; they won't want a fight. If we fire a few shots over their heads, they'll go back quicker than they came; there's no need for bloodshed.' Daniel was almost pleading.

'Well, that's not your decision is it? Like I said, I'm the boss. No, this time we teach them a lesson, let them come in then we give it to them, Smith get them ready.'

'Mister Dobson, should we put the torches out on the caves, so they can't see what's going on?' Smith asked.

'No, keep the torches alight, anything that brings those revenue scums right to us.' Dobson knew what he was doing.

Dobson strode away as Smith started shouting, looking in particular at Daniel, 'So, if there's no one else scared to fight, prime your muskets and get ready, they're coming this way!' He pointed at the path.

Meanwhile, the Duty Men were exhausted, led by Hardwicke they had walked up the steep path much too fast, they were out of breath and sweating in their heavy woollen uniform tunics, some were using the butts of their muskets as walking sticks to help walk up the steep incline.

'Sir, may I suggest we rest up a bit and give the men a chance to recover and prepare themselves before we meet whatever is up there?' Sergeant Tinsley asked.

'Nonsense, Sergeant, this is our chance to wipe out these smugglers once and for all, can't you see the lights up ahead. Let's get after them now while we have the chance!' Hardwicke was excited and he was right, up on top of the West Hill were lights and plenty of them, some stationary, some moving, but there was activity on the hill this night and as Tinsley saw the same lights, he became more nervous of what was to come.

'Sir, this is too obvious, it may be a ruse or a trap we're walking into?' Tinsley could hear himself almost pleading with Hardwicke; every part of him knew this night would end badly.

Hardwicke stopped walking causing Tinsley and the men behind him to crash into one another in an almost comedic fashion. Turning to look at Tinsley, Hardwicke was in no mood for observations and concerns about his leadership.

'Sergeant Tinsley, you and the men will obey my orders or you will be clapped in irons like any common criminal on a charge of cowardice, now get the men to load and prime their muskets, we will drive these smuggling scum from Hastings this night, do I make myself clear?' His face was almost touching Tinsley's as he growled the words at him.

'Very good, sir. You heard the Captain, men; load and prime your muskets!' Tinsley barked the order.

The men started loading their muskets, tired, nervous and inexperienced; some of them dropped their ramrods in their panic, they double-loaded their barrels with two musket balls or forgot to prime the pan of their weapons with gun powder. Once loaded, they continued up the path. Out of ten men, probably only half of the muskets with them would fire properly.

Back at the top of the West Hill, the team of enforcers were either kneeling or lying down, muskets pointed at the path. Daniel was used to waiting in the dark for the enemy. He had done it so many times before when he was serving in Spain. His eyes had become fully accustomed to the dark and he felt that he could see anything that would come his way. It was then that he heard someone walking behind him. Turning quickly, he pointed his musket at the figure standing over him; Daniel, after years in the army was alert to movement, noise and light.

'What's the matter, soldier boy, are you scared?' It was Smith; he had obviously taken a disliking to Daniel after his question to Dobson.

'Me being scared doesn't matter, it's what's over there that is the problem. Get down, take cover, shut your mouth and look that way.' Daniel pointed at the path.

Smith surprised himself by doing what he was told, staring as Daniel had told him there was movement, listening for the noise of people walking, even the sound of voices. Then they came, a group of about a dozen men; the Duty Men were very close to their position and, by the manner of their movement, were completely unaware of what they were walking into.

'Well, well, soldier boy; you were right!' Then he was away, crouching, running and talking to each of his men.

Hardwicke was so intent on getting to the torches that lit up the top of the West Hill that he couldn't see what was directly in front of him. He had mouthed an instruction at Tinsley so that the Duty Men were fanned out from single file into a kind of skirmish line; little did they know that this was to the advantage of the men lying in wait for them.

Daniel could see them coming. Closer and closer the Duty Men got, inside his heart he was raging, 'what is wrong with you, do you want to die?' He asked them silently.

As the Duty Men crested the hill, they could see the many torches lighting up the caves and for the first time they could see people, lots of them, brazenly moving around the now illuminated carts making no attempt to conceal themselves.

'Halt,' Tinsley ordered and the men stopped their ascent.

Before Hardwicke could say anything, Tinsley made his case; he knew everything was wrong about this operation. 'I tell you now, Captain, look for yourself there are too many of them, we can't take them on.'

'Sergeant Tinsley, they are a disorganised rabble of thugs. We will fire them a volley and they'll scatter like dust, then we charge them. As for you, after this night's insubordination, you are relieved of your rank. Follow me, men.' Onwards they marched, all the men had witnessed the exchange between their superiors and all wished that they were anywhere but on the West Hill in the middle of the night.

Daniel's heart was beating so fast he had trouble keeping his breath, not because he was scared but because he knew he would have a hand in a slaughter. The Duty Men were less than fifty paces from the enforcers when Daniel made his decision, aiming above the Duty Men he fired his musket in the air to warn them away. There was the flash of the musket firing from the pan as the powder was ignited then a second flash and a bang as the musket ball flew out of the barrel of his Charleville. In the dark, no one could make out who fired their musket, Smith swore and shouted, 'Fire!'

The enforcers fired their muskets, they were no better than thugs with muskets, several Duty Men fell backwards, the rest were still standing, but the volley had its effect as they fired their muskets off in a panicked reply. Two of the enforcers were hit and fell down where they stood.

Captain Hardwicke shouted at his men to charge, two of them turned and ran away in the opposite direction, Hardwicke, sword drawn, ran forward with Sergeant Tinsley and what was left of his men, they were all doomed. Daniel having fired his musket, did what years of experience taught him to do, he had it reloaded in seconds. He could see the charge by the Duty Men was half-hearted; they were slow apart from an officer, whom he recognized as he carried a sword. This officer was running straight at him. 'You fool,' he muttered to himself. He fired at the officer from only ten paces, the musket ball hitting the man in the chest with a thump. He exhaled in the most unnatural manner and was lifted up and flung backwards, landing in an undignified heap; he was dead immediately.

Tinsley saw Hardwicke go down and wanted to shout retreat to the remnants of his men but it was too late, young Stark was beside him screaming as they ran, whether from fear or to frighten the enemy he couldn't tell, then whoosh, the young man's face exploded as a musket ball hit him between the eyes and he was dead.

Amidst the noise of musket fire, Daniel recognised a voice. 'Now, boys, let's have 'em!' It was Dobson, who ran past him holding some type of club with Harrison close behind him. That was it; the enforcers followed their leader and hit the exhausted Duty Men as a hammer hits an anvil. It was no fight, it was a massacre; the Duty Men were outnumbered and no match for the group of thugs who clubbed them with their muskets and tore into them with knives. The most fearsome was Harrison; out of the corner of his eye Daniel, saw him hit a Duty Man with a punch that knocked him senseless before he was mobbed by the other enforcers. There was one Duty Man who knew how to fight though, Tinsley, he hadn't fired his musket off, he knew what was coming and dropped one of the enforcers with a perfect shot in the chest as the thug ran at him, no time to reload he turned the musket butt end forward and hit another man who was trying to club him.

Dobson loved a good fight and, seeing the one Duty Man with some mettle, he thought, 'He's mine!'

Dobson ran at the Duty Man, screaming, and brought his club downwards to smash the man's skull. Tinsley parried the club with his musket, then, in lighting speed, swiveled the musket down and around to hit the man across the jaw.

Dobson flew backwards as blood and several teeth shot out of his mouth, lying on his back he could see the Duty Man standing over him musket butt facing down towards him ready to smash his head in. As the musket butt lifted, the Duty Man was hit by something and fell down.

Daniel had picked up a cudgel dropped by one of Dobson's enforcers; as the Duty Man tried to get up, he swung it again and hit him hard across the chest, knocking him flat.

Daniel held the Duty Man down. 'Stay down and live, or try to get up and die a hero. Make your choice.'

As Tinsley closed his eyes and played dead, Daniel turned his attention back to Dobson and offered his hand. The fight was over, all the Duty Men were down and it was a horrible scene as the group of enforcers howled in their victory, waving their muskets and clubs in the air.

Taking Daniel's hand, Dobson got up, spitting blood out of his mouth. 'Who are you?'

'My name is Sibson,' answered Daniel.

'Sibson? Well, you know how to fight,' Dobson said, then he walked off to take charge again.

The noise of the fight had brought all the other men from the West Hill and now a large crowd gathered around the path that was littered with the bodies of the dead.

Dobson had a full audience now and he would not miss this chance to bathe in his own glory. 'This was a new bunch of Duty Men, them and their captain made a big mistake and underestimated us and now they've paid the price and are all dead. So, there it is, boys; no one messes with our operation!'

There were cheers and Dobson was happy with his speech. As the smugglers reveled in their victory, Sergeant Tinsley seized his chance to crawl away into the darkness and save his life.

'Right, enough time wasted, we'll have their weapons, belts, and boots, anything you can use. Leave them where they lay as a gift for our esteemed magistrate!'

They all laughed. Daniel didn't laugh, in fact he felt sick, he thought he had finished killing when he left the army. As for Captain Hardwicke and the dead Duty Men there was no dignity; their dead bodies were handled roughly, turned over and spread where they were stripped of everything apart from their shirts and breeches. Daniel felt sick to the pit of his stomach, his legs went weak and he put his hand over his mouth fearing he would vomit. Images of Waterloo flashed through his mind as he stood looking at the dead Duty Men; this night was never meant to end this way. There was a feeling that someone was looking at him, as though a pair of eyes were burning into his head. He turned and found Ralph beside him with a horrified look on his face.

'My God, Daniel, what have you done?'

'I don't know, Ralph, I don't know.' Daniel shook his head and, throwing the Charleville on the ground, walked away.

It was a windy morning with dark clouds gathered over the West Hill as Sir John Rutherford sat on his horse; his head hung low and he felt depressed as he watched the Hastings parish vicar, Mister Higgs, make his prayers over the body of Captain Hardwicke. Standing beside Sir John's horse was

Doctor Gibson, the only surgeon in Hastings. Gibson had finished examining the last of the dead Duty Men, who had all now been lined in a row, their dignity restored with calico blankets thrown over them. As Gibson poured water from a pitcher over his hands to wash the blood from them, he too watched the vicar go about his work.

'Well, Sir John, prayers are the least we can do for them, but they can't have died in vain.' Doctor Gibson's words cut Sir John to the bone.

Both men then saw a horse and cart come up the road, as it drew closer they could see it carried Tappin and one of his watchmen. As the cart stopped close to him Sir John could feel anger welling up from his stomach to his heart.

Tappin attempted to say, 'Good morning, gentl…'

'Tell me you had no hand in this murder, in this massacre, Tappin. Tell me the truth! Swear it or, by God, I'll have you hung! Do you hear me, man?' Sir John was incandescent with anger.

Tappin started blubbering, so nervous he could hardly get his words out. 'Sir John, no of course not, I heard the firing and the shouting, by the time I got up here with my men, it was all over, I swear!'

Sir John was in no way pacified by Tappin's answer. 'Tappin, I promise I will get to the root of last night's murder. If I find you are involved, you will swing from a rope! Now get out of my sight!'

Tappin was only too pleased to leave, tapping the reins and touching the horse with his whip; the cart turned and was gone. The annoyance departed, Sir John looked back at the row of dead bodies. He shook his head as he surveyed the scene of carnage on the West Hill. 'I told him to wait, I told him I would get him more men. Damn it damn it, he led them into a trap and in they marched like lambs to the slaughter, their deaths were completely unnecessary!'

'So what is to be done then, Sir John?' asked Gibson.

'I will tell you what is to be done, Doctor Gibson. First, we will speak to the lone survivor you treated at the Martello Tower this morning. Next, anything we talk about or do from this point on will stay between us.'

Gibson nodded.

'Then you and I will be travelling to London. We cannot do this by ourselves; if they will kill Duty Men like this, what can they get up to next? I will write to London today. I know people in the government, we will state our case there. At this rate, they will bleed the town – nay, the whole county – dry.'

Gibson smiled sarcastically. 'London, what can London do for Hastings?'

'Our challenge is to find experienced, honest men to do a job. There is only one way to do that, they have to be men who don't come from Hastings. I have men in mind that I served with in Spain, we have to write letters now, we will not go to London with an empty hand of cards, nor do I intend to leave with an empty purse, I bid you good day Doctor Gibson!'

Pulling on the reins Sir John turned his mount, kicking his heels he rode his horse as fast away from the West Hill as it would carry him. As the horse galloped, Sir John still felt angry but he was also exhilarated, a plan was forming in his mind and he knew just the people to carry it out.

Chapter Two
The Good Life

A new lodgings and regular money, Daniel was feeling good about his life as he looked in a small cracked mirror stuck on the wall of the room he and Ralph now lived in above Bill Crisp's shop. How different he looked from the disheveled veteran of a few weeks before. Pulling a new jacket onto his shoulders he admired the garment and his own clean shaven face. Still looking in the mirror, he could see Ralph sitting on the bed with an expression on his face that was not one of admiration of his friend. Since the fight on the hill with the Duty Men, Ralph had gone into a solemn mood, he ate little, said little, in fact he did little of anything. Daniel had carried on for days as if everything was fine but his friend's depression had peeved him to the point of anger and he turned about aggressively to face Ralph and have things out.

'Damn it, Ralph, what is it? You've been sitting on that bed all morning with a face like a slapped backside! What is it, man? Speak up!'

Startled by Daniel's outburst, Ralph sat bolt upright. He had an opportunity to vent and now he would do it. 'What do you think, Daniel? Look at you preening yourself in your fine new clothes like a prize cockerel, bought with the money you made from killing those Duty Men on the hill. How can you live with yourself?'

'Of course, you are my conscience, Ralph. Whatever I do must have your leave, is that it?'

'No, it's not that, Daniel. Smuggling barrels of gin I can do; killing servants of the crown is another matter.'

Daniel wanted to shout at Ralph but paused and caught his breath for a moment, controlling his breathing he walked over to the bed and leaned down.

'Here's the thing Ralph, we have a roof over our heads, food and drink, coin in the pockets of our new clothes and we don't stink like a herd of swine any more. Do you really think I wanted to kill that officer up on the hill? Let me answer for you; of course I didn't but you know what, if I have to do things to survive and live a half-decent life, I will and if you don't like it, there's the door!'

Now Daniel was panting, he wasn't used to arguing with his old friend like this. Ralph had stood up in the middle of the tirade and both men were face-to-face.

Ralph said nothing but picked up his coat from the bed behind him and walked over to the door and opened it. 'You're right, Daniel, I have no right to judge you. Come on, let's go to work.' He lifted his eyes in the air as he said the last word.

Shaking his head, Daniel followed him out the door.

Dobson owned a building in the town a short walk from Crisp's shop; it was worst kept secret in Hastings. Whilst it appeared to the outside as an old fisherman's home, grey, dull and empty, the inside was another story. Dobson ran his town operation from the house. Amongst the gang, it was known as the "depot". Any person in the town knew not to use the front door but the alley at the back of the house. It was busy, people came there to buy what they could and for Dobson it was another money earner away from the contraband he sent all over the south of the country. There was constant movement between the contraband he stored in the caves and the depot where he would move his goods from. After the fight on the hill Dobson had made it clear to Watson he wanted Daniel working in the depot whenever he needed him. When Watson had told Daniel this, he agreed, but with one condition which was that Ralph had to come with him. Dobson must have agreed because, like many mornings before, Daniel and Ralph were there with coats off, moving crates and keeping the shop operation supplied.

While he worked Daniel looked at the characters around him and sized them up in his own way. While Smith was loud, bullish, arrogant and full of himself, Harrison was everything the opposite in his personality. Harrison said little, he kept himself to himself but Daniel could see he was a real fighter. A tough man never has to tell anyone how tough he is, he just is. Daniel had seen enough of them in his life. Dobson was right about him, Harrison was tall, strong and fit, an obvious prize fighter, his nose was still straight but he had scars around his eyes and cheekbones and his hands were massive. Daniel could see that Harrison was just like himself – he did what he had to do to survive. Daniel was also conscious of how people felt towards him and the feeling was one of hostility. Where Smith and Watson were obviously jealous of Daniel's new found favour with Dobson, Harrison made no comment. If anything, he was cordial to Daniel in his own way and showed kindness to Ralph.

As the men worked, Smith, as usual, was throwing his weight around, shouting and manhandling people he accused of slacking but really because he liked doing it, that was what made a bully happy. Despite his one arm, Ralph worked as hard as any other man and had his own way of pulling small barrels up and onto his shoulder. Another barrel heaved onto his shoulder Ralph walked out to a waiting cart in the alley outside. Smith, supervising the loading of the cart, watched him and smiled to himself with a glint of nasty mischief in his eye. Standing by the cart, Smith timed his nastiness to perfection; as the one-armed veteran approached, he put his foot out and tripped Ralph, sending him sprawling forwards onto his face, the barrel smashing on the cobbled road with the contents of tobacco wrapped in cloth thrown everywhere.

'Silly boy, you should be more careful. If that tobacco's ruined, it will come out of your pay,' Smith laughed.

Ralph was stood up in a second, face-to-face with his assailant, but Smith reacted quickly and pushed him back, sending Ralph on to the ground for the second time.

Smith stood over Ralph. 'You soldier boy, you think we owe you something, no one gives a damn about your battles in Spain, Waterloo wherever the hell it was.'

The whole thing was seen by Daniel who made straight for his friend's attacker but it was Harrison who beat him to it and squared up to Smith. Smith wasn't smirking any more – he hadn't reckoned on dealing with a real fighter and took a step back away from Harrison, trying to keep face in front of the watching eyes around him.

'This is not your fight, Harrison, so stay out of it,' he uttered, but Harrison, who was as usual silent, stared, but his silence was resounding in its own way.

Harrison felt a hand on his shoulder; it was Ralph.

'Stand fast, Harrison, I can deal with Smith; another bully who thinks he can push people around.'

As Harrison stepped aside, Smith opened his mouth to utter another insult to Ralph, but he hadn't reckoned on a fight straight away. As Ralph squared up to Smith he kicked him with all the force of his right boot between his legs. Smith, wheezing in agony, bent over, hands between his legs, then Ralph pulled Smith's head low with his good arm and kneed him in the face with his left knee. Smith changed direction in an instant and went backwards, his head flying up with blood spurting out of his nose and mouth; he collapsed in a coughing, bloody heap on the floor, not knowing whether to hold his face or his organs.

Ralph stood over him. 'Smith, if you ever touch me again, lay a hand on me or cross me in any way, it won't be a bloody nose or bruising to your genitals you'll have to worry about.'

Smith was in too much agony and surprise to reply. He just stared at Ralph, astonished by what had happened to him.

Ralph walked away with Daniel. Harrison lifted Smith up and did something people rarely saw him do: he smiled. Daniel helped his friend pick up the mess from the smashed barrel and within a moment, crates and barrels were back moving again. As for Smith, the bully had been out-bullied. Those involved in the incident were completely unaware that Dobson and his man Watson had seen the whole thing. As things returned to normal, he spoke some words into Watson's ear and walked away, leaving Watson to stare at Daniel and Ralph. As if the morning had not been interesting enough something else happened that would make the day even more memorable for Daniel.

A couple of hours after the brawl, a horse and carriage arrived, the driver was a very old man but it was the passenger that caught Daniel's eye. A young woman, or, to be more exact, a young lady, who was truly beautiful, sat in the back; she was educated and well-dressed, like any society lady.

'What was she doing in the fishing village?' Daniel asked himself.

The driver was infirm on his feet and was barely able to get off his seat to climb down and pull the steps out for the beauty to step down onto the ground. Dobson came out from the building and hugged the woman as only a father would. His eyes sparkled as he looked at her; it was obvious Dobson was holding his daughter. Daniel was awoken from his trance by a slap on his back, it was Watson.

'Close your mouth, Sibson, spit is drooling out of your mouth and you look like an imbecile,' Watson sneered.

Embarrassed at being caught so obviously staring at the young lady, Daniel felt his face turn red but thought it better to say nothing.

'When you finish your work stay here, the boss wants to see you. Just you mind you send your one armed friend home, have you got that?'

'Aye, I have,' Daniel answered.

Seeing the exchange, Ralph was curious.

'What was that about?' Ralph asked.

'The boss wants to see me when I finish. What for, I know not.'

'Well, Daniel, remember the words of Homer: beware the Greeks bearing gifts.'

'I remember in Spain you were always reading Ralph, and, as for me, I have no idea what you are talking about!'

They both laughed.

As instructed, Daniel stayed behind when the others had gone home. He was ushered into a room by Watson, where he found Dobson sitting at a table with his ever-present shadow, Harrison, standing behind him. This was the nearest he had ever been to Dobson since he saved his life on the West Hill. Neither man spoke as Dobson eyed Daniel up and down.

Dobson was used to intimidating anyone he spoke to before starting a conversation, it gave him the advantage in whatever followed but in Daniel he sensed no fear. In fact, he sensed nothing.

'So, you are Daniel Sibson, the man who stopped my brains from being smashed in by a musket butt. Tell me of yourself. Where you are from, what have you done?'

'That may take some time, Mister Dobson.'

'I run everything in Hastings, even time. Get on with it,' Dobson was a man comfortable in his power.

Daniel did as he was told. As he spoke of his time in the army, it was the first time he had ever gone back in his mind over how things had happened and he surprised himself with everything he had done.

After some minutes, Dobson raised his hand, interrupting Daniel in mid-flow.

'I've heard enough. So a little bird tells me you took an interest in my daughter?'

Feeling complete embarrassment, Daniel kept silent.

'I will tell you something that few others will ever hear, that girl is everything to me, that's all you need to know. But it won't surprise you I have enemies, lots of them and they will do anything they can to hurt me. Harrison here keeps an eye on me but you saw the doddery old fool who drives my girl around, he couldn't protect himself never mind her.'

'What is it you need, Mister Dobson?' Daniel wanted to get to the nub of the conversation.

'You know, Sibson, if any other talked to me like that, I would split them like a piece of mackerel, but that's why you're here, you have guts. Here's the thing; as of tomorrow, you will be my daughter's driver. You will take her wherever she needs to go. Her name is Laura and she keeps herself busy. You will collect her in the morning from my home in Battle and bring her back when she is done. Just you keep her safe and keep your paws to yourself, otherwise I'll have Harrison here beat you to a pulp. Watson will sort out the carriage for you and the arrangements. Now get out.'

Daniel knew that was how Dobson was; there was no choice in things. He told his men to do things and expected it done, so he just left and waited for Watson to instruct him.

The next morning, Daniel found himself sitting in a decent horse and carriage, admiring the beautiful, undulating fields of East Sussex. In the foreground, he could see the outer walls of Battle Abbey, built on the field where the battle of Hastings took place all those years before. Turning away from the abbey, he looked at Dobson's home, a fine house just outside the town of Battle with land and servants attending to the house and manning the fields. For the innocent eye, one would think it the home of a gentrified land owner, not a ruthless leader of a criminal gang. At nine o'clock sharp, Dobson came out of the house with Laura. Just like the day before, Daniel felt a murmuring in his heart. That girl was a thing of beauty; it wasn't just her looks, she exuded charm and grace.

'Laura, this is Sibson, your new driver. I have old Wilf doing other things, he will take you to your different charities or whatever it is you do.'

Laura said nothing but looked Daniel up and down, kissed her father and climbed into the carriage, helped up by her new driver. As the carriage pulled away, Dobson pointed at his own eyes and then at Daniel in a manner of "my eyes are on you".

Laura made no conversation except to tell Daniel where to go. Dobson was true to his words, Laura did keep herself busy, reading with her ladies groups, piano lessons and a number of local charities that she worked on as a leading donor and organiser. Thinking about the business her father was involved in made Daniel smile to himself as he found hypocrisy amusing. For several days Daniel did as he was bid by Dobson and drove Laura all around Hastings, Bexhill and Rye. Apart from a "Good morning" and "Wait here", there was little or no conversation initiated by Laura. This changed when Daniel brought Laura to her most precious undertaking, an orphanage in Bexhill. On this morning, Laura's basket was bulging as she came out of the house and with good reason; she had brought bread for the children. The orphanage was made up of several grey brick buildings set in some land away from the town. If the buildings looked dull from the outside, then inside the main hall, where the children sat on the floor in ordered rows, was forbidding and miserable, suitable for providing a roof over the children's head and nothing else. As for the children, they were dressed in rags and looked starving.

The workers stood at the edges of the hall around the children like prison guards; they were intimidating and had a look of cruelty on their faces. For the past few days Daniel had stopped looking at Laura as a beautiful young woman and instead thought her the spoilt brat of a nasty criminal trying to salve her conscience with acts of kindness. Carrying the basket with bread, Daniel stood behind Laura as she handed buns to the poor emaciated children sitting on the floor. A brief glimmer of happiness came to their faces as they started eating their food straight away. Watching the children Daniel smiled, happy to see them eat, he had been hungry himself as a child and understood their pain and loneliness but he felt no happiness as he watched the reaction of the workers. If anything, they appeared jealous and angry about this act of giving that helped the children. Daniel feared what would happen to the children once he drove Miss Laura away in her smart carriage and finery. As he looked at the rags the children were dressed in and their sad eyes staring out from their thin, gaunt faces, he wondered, as he often did, why he had spent fifteen years killing the French all over Europe. What did it really achieve if children in England were still starving hungry?

As Laura gave more bread to the children, Daniel noticed something: tears. Laura said nothing but tears ran down her face as she went from child to child, these were genuine emotions as though she knew this small kindness was almost a token effort and these innocents needed much more help.

One little girl, so hungry as she tried to force the bread down her throat, started coughing, almost choking; a boy next to her patted her back, but one of the orphanage workers was less gentle. A rough-looking man picked up the girl by the scruff, shouting at her.

'Stupid child, you can't even eat properly!' He hit her violently on the back with a stick he was holding, the girl screamed in pain, arched her back and dropped to the floor, rolling and crying in agony. Laura had seen the whole thing and covered her mouth with her hand, in shock, as the man stood over the child, stick raised to hit her again.

Smack! A punch hit the man straight on the chin, landing him flat on his backside. Still dazed, the bully now turned coward, shrinking back in fear as Daniel picked him up by his jacket, ready to punch him again.

'Daniel! No, that's enough!' It was Laura.

Pulling the man's face close to his own Daniel hissed at him. 'I will come back to this place every week. If I see a mark on that little girl or any other child, I swear to God I will break every bone on your body. Do you hear me?'

As Daniel threw the man to the floor, he curled up in a ball, crying as all bullies do when confronted. By now Laura had picked up the little girl and hugged her, rubbing her back, she walked away and spoke to a woman, presumably the governess in charge of the orphanage and handed the child to her.

Normality returned quickly and Laura continued on her mission with Daniel following behind. Their work done, Daniel went to leave with Laura but saw the girl he had protected earlier looking at him. Walking across to her, she was so minute that he had to lean down on his haunches to speak with her.

'What's your name, little miss?'

'Me, sir? My name is Maria.'

As Daniel listened to her, he could see there wasn't a bad bone in her body.

'From whence do you come, little Miss Maria?'

'Why, I think from Hastings, sir, but I can only remember living here,' she answered with no malice in her expression or voice.

Daniel could feel himself grimace as she spoke the words, but made himself smile for her.

'Do you have any sisters or brothers, Miss Maria?' Daniel asked.

'I did, sir, but they're with Jesus now, as are my mother and father.'

His heart sinking, Daniel smiled again and patted little Maria on the head.

'Well, Miss Maria, my name is Daniel and I look forward to seeing you the next time I come with bread, now you run along with your friends.'

'That will be nice, Mister Daniel, bye bye.' Maria lifted her tiny hand and waved it at Daniel, she then skipped away to join the other children. Daniel stayed kneeling watching her as she ran away and unconsciously shook his head at her and the whole situation the children were in.

Twenty minutes later, sitting in the carriage outside the orphanage, Laura fiddled with the contents of her bag. Without looking up, she spoke. 'I understand your anger, Daniel, but violence is not the answer.'

'I know, Miss Laura, and I'm very sorry for that; it was just when I saw that thug beating the child I couldn't control myself.'

'You are from Hastings, Daniel?'

'Yes, I was just like the children we saw there. I never knew my parents, I was brought up by an aunt, long since dead. Then I joined the army.'

'Why did you enlist in the army, Daniel?'

'Because I had nothing else here, the fishing work was piecemeal and I wanted to get away, all these years later here I am back.'

'Back and working as a common criminal, not such a homecoming for a hero of Waterloo.' Laura might have been toying with her driver but her remark had gone too far and Daniel smarted at the arrogance the words contained.

'What gives you the right to judge me? How do you think you are wearing these fine clothes and having your sowing afternoons with your rich lady friends in Battle?'

Laura was not used to people talking back to her; she was on the back foot and flustered. Laura tried to control the conversation, using her father as a stick.

'How dare you speak to me like that! I could have my father throw you out of Hastings!'

Before she could finish, Daniel butted in.

'Then have him throw me out, but I won't be judged by you. The only reason you're sitting there, safe and sound in all your finery, is because people like me were dying and bleeding over there in Europe, otherwise you'd be speaking French with your lady friends now. As for Waterloo, the only heroes are the ten thousand dead men we left there!'

'The cheek of it, you and all those other ruffians working for my father are nothing but fiends, you do not have the sense to realise that one day this will all come to an end!'

'Oh really, I disgust you, well I don't see you complaining at the wealth and the life your father and us fiends have given you!'

Laura caught her breath and looked around before answering; Daniel had a point.

'Yes, my father does what he must; it doesn't mean I'm like him does it! You're all the same, you think you're so clever, but all you're doing is sucking the life out of everyone, bleeding people dry until there's nothing left for anyone.' Laura was angry and upset but could feel hypocrisy in her own words as she defended her corner.

'I am born as I am, but I assure you my luck, my privilege will be used for a better cause than smuggling.'

Daniel knew he had landed more blows that he had taken, that was enough foolish conversation.

'If you're quite finished, where to, Miss Laura?' He turned and faced back towards the horses at the front drawing the carriage. Laura was flushed deep red and speechless.

She coughed then recomposed herself.' Take me home, please.'

With a flick of the riding whip, the horses set off and they travelled back to the house in Battle. As they arrived outside the large front door of the house, Daniel jumped off his seat and pulled the carriage footstep down; he held his hand out for Laura who stepped down off the carriage; as she took his hand, their eyes met.

'Daniel, forgive me, I had no right to judge you.'

'Miss Laura, you are you and I am me, there's nothing further to talk about.'

Feeling her face heat up again, Laura looked down; letting go of his hand, she walked away into the house as a waiting maid curtsied and opened the door for her.

Chapter Three
London

Captain Munro felt awkward. He was unused to sitting in government offices in London, but here he was, in a fine building in Whitehall, sitting outside the Home Secretary's office for what purpose, he knew not. Since returning from the war he had spent his time working on the family estate in Hampshire, keeping to himself and avoiding any conversation of matters related to fighting Napoleon. The exile was now over for Munro, he sat once again in his dusted-off officer's uniform with the tight fitting high collar that itched his neck; sword and scabbard touching the floor, he held the hilt nervously to his hip. What was he doing here?

A man in the uniform of a Royal Navy Captain sat opposite him, looking equally uncomfortable and ill at ease. Munro noticed the navy man was clutching a letter; it looked very similar to the one he had received from Sir John Rutherford.

Inside the Home Secretary's office a loud, animated discussion was taking place and Sir John Rutherford was in full flow. 'Home Secretary, I have ten men of the Preventative Service murdered and not one person held to account! How bad should the situation be?'

'My question to you, Sir John, would be how could this be allowed to go on?' The Home Secretary knew the answer to his question but wanted to hear the words for himself from the Hastings Magistrate.

'These people are organised, they have informants, corrupt officials and traders, we must destroy them first and then go after any person or anything that has supported, met, traded or benefitted in any way from them.'

'Cut to the quick, Sir John. What are you asking for? The military?' the Home Secretary asked.

'No, Home Secretary, I do not expect or want a regiment of foot guards, but the Preventative Service and voluntary yeomanry are not enough on their own, both need experienced officers and veterans from the war to lead them that cannot be bought by smugglers who have guineas to spare.'

'Forgive me, Sir John, I am aware of your situation and was toying with you somewhat but more seriously; I wanted to understand the level of criminality involved by speaking with you directly. No further explanation is required, yours is not the only coastal town that is plagued with this lawlessness; Kent, Hampshire, Dorset, the problem has grown and continues to grow as we speak. Yours is not the first complaint on this matter, while we were busy fighting Napoleon, they were building their trade right under our noses, you will not be surprised to know that His Majesty's Treasury is losing thousands of pounds because of this illicit trade, the effects go well beyond our coastal towns believe me, this will be a case of the ends justifies the means.'

Sir John held his breath, realising that he no longer had to convince the Home Secretary for help, held his peace.

'So, what have you in mind, Sir John?'

'What I have in mind is waiting outside. With your permission?'

The Home Secretary nodded his head and waved his arm to his waiting secretary who went to the door.

The discussion was loud enough that Munro and the naval officer could make out some words. At that moment, the door opened and the typical government civil servant with round spectacles, black suit and a high collar walked out.

'Captain Munro, Captain Townsend, the Home Secretary and Sir John will see you now.'

Walking into the Home Secretary's office the secretary directed the men to chairs at a table directly opposite Sir John and the Home Secretary. The two military men recognised Sir John and both unconsciously nodded acknowledgement to him.

'Gentlemen, you may or may not know me; my name is Sir Robert Steele, the Home Secretary of the government. I thank you both for coming here this day; I understand you are both former colleagues of Sir John. We have a proposition for you, but first Sir John will tell you why you are here and what he intends for you. Sir John?'

Sir John first introduced both officers to the Home Secretary and it was an opportunity for both men to find out about each other.

The Naval Captain was called Townsend and he was a veteran of the Battle of Trafalgar amongst other sea actions. From the outside people thought he was angry, he wasn't angry, he was just a man who did things properly, his uniform, drills, everything. He expected the same from his officers, sailors and marines, no more no less, he was firm but fair. This was also how he came across during conversations. Like Munro, Sir John knew him from the war.

Sir John then spoke for some minutes, telling both men about the massacre on the West Hill and what was behind it.

The magistrate was honest. 'The problem, gentlemen, is that they are not helping people; they are the strong preying on the weak. Theirs is not a victimless crime, they are bleeding the town and, for that matter, East Sussex dry. It's quite simple, I want them stopped. This goes far beyond a few barrels of tea; they have no regard for law and order and why should they? The Town Constable, the Duty Men, they are scared witless of them and with good reason; these men are killers. If we are to stop them, it will be akin to going to war.'

'Allow me to speak plainly, Sir John. I, we, can fix this problem, but this can be done only if you can give me the men and authority, must I explain more?' Captain Munro asked looking at both Sir John and the Home Secretary.

The Home Secretary interjected. 'You will make an example in Hastings, and once Hastings is fixed the message will be clear to the others, your trade and its end is nigh. I will give you what you need but make this work!'

Townsend had kept silent but it was his turn to speak, 'Sir John, if it is to be a war so be it, I can do that as can my men, my only condition is that I have your support but also that of London and the government but I warn you locking a few of them up will make no difference, what will the support be?'

'I cannot promise you a "Man o War", but you will have resources, both of you. Recruit men you can trust, this is not about ships or muskets but about integrity and a willingness to deal with the problem. You will find the men you need and plan your operation with Sir John as your commander. I am fed up to the back teeth of hearing about Hastings – and East Sussex, for that matter – and these damn smugglers and their menacing ways. I want rid of them, once and for all!'

The Home Secretary had made his intentions very clear and there was no more to be said. Sir John shook hands with the Home Secretary thanking him; he and the two officers were then ushered out of the office by the secretary. Once outside, Sir John had a chance to speak plainly with Munro and Townsend.

'Well, gentlemen, there it is. If you want no involvement in this enterprise, walk away now; if you're in, my club in Pall Mall serves a decent lunch.'

After a short pause Townsend said, 'I'm Royal Navy, I trust there's fish and a good red wine on the menu?'

'I don't care what's on the menu; all this stuff with government buildings and Home Secretary business has given me a hell of an appetite!' Munro suggested and then all three men laughed and went to get their overcoats.

The lunch at the Reform Club was not a disappointment. Townsend had his fish and red wine which were also enjoyed by Munro and Sir John. The three veterans were getting on well; as they were drinking their second glass of after-dinner port, Sir John decided that the reliving of memories fighting Napoleon had run its course and it was now time to get down to business.

'So, gentlemen, I think that's enough of the war for now. You know full well that I have brought you on board as I know you both well from Spain and Belgium, and for yourself, Townsend, from Egypt and the Mediterranean.'

Munro and Townsend put their brains into military mode and stayed silent waiting for the rest of the briefing.

'You heard quite a bit when we met the Home Secretary but I withheld some parts of the situation more from embarrassment. I would describe our smuggling gang in Hastings as hiding in plain sight. The hill where the Duty Men were murdered has a series of caves where they stash their ill-gotten gains; they even have a building in Hastings town where they trade from with no fear of intervention from the law. I need you both to recruit your own men, veterans that have the guts to go into these places, men who can't be intimidated or for that matter bought.'

Townsend thought for a moment on Sir John's words.

'Fighting in the caves and streets I can do, but I'm a Navy man; what do you want me to do?'

'That's a good question; let me discuss your roles in more detail. I want you, Townsend, to take direct command of the Hastings Preventative Service, by all means recruit some of your veterans from Trafalgar and America but I also want you to raise the morale of the survivors left over after the massacre, they are leaderless and rudderless at the moment. Anything to do with water is yours: the sea, harbours, anything.'

'That's fine, Sir John.' Townsend nodded as he answered.

'Munro, you are in charge of intelligence. You have carte blanche authority to use whatever measures are necessary to build up intelligence on this criminal scum. Again, you will take command of the Volunteer Yeomanry Cavalry they are based in the town of Battle but are next to useless. Get some veterans in and train up the yeomanry to a fighting standard. I want you both to coordinate your efforts. When between you there is enough intelligence, hit them hard, very hard!'

'I can do that, Sir John, as I'm sure Captain Townsend can, but how long do we have before you expect some outcomes?' Munro asked.

'Today's lunch was the easy bit. I expect to see you both in Hastings in two weeks with men recruited and the start of a plan.'

There were no comments just accepting gestures that they understood.

'One more thing, Townsend; there was a survivor from the West Hill. A Sergeant Tinsley. He needs lifting up, I'm sure you understand what I mean.' Sir John gave Townsend a knowing look as he lifted his glass of port.

'I understand perfectly, Sir John,' Townsend answered as he and Munro clinked glasses with Sir John.

Several weeks had passed since Daniel and Laura had had their argument. Much as he tried to deny it to himself; Daniel was upset and disappointed because deep down he wanted to get on with Laura, not just because she was beautiful but that she was genuine in her concern for others and he liked this. Days of driving her became drudgery: no conversation, no niceties, just orders of where to go and when to collect. Mulling this over, Daniel stared at the last drop of ale in his tankard as his days had become routine, collect Miss Laura drive her around the county, take her home then spend the evening in the Sailor's Tavern in Hastings town watching the rest of the gang and poor Ralph in particular, drink themselves into oblivion. Daniel didn't drink as much as the others but the alternative was to sit in the room he and Ralph shared above Crisp's shop and die of boredom, so it was better to get out. As the main tavern in Hastings, the "Sailor's" was packed with locals and travellers, as it was on most evenings. As Daniel turned to the buxom young woman standing behind the counter to get his tankard refilled, he thought he had seen a ghost. Dressed in a long waxed riding coat a man sat by himself at a table nursing a large tankard of beer; he looked around and stared hard at Daniel then turned his attention back to the tankard taking a swig from it. Daniel and the solitary figure recognised each other straight away. As if there was some understanding between them both men then proceeded to ignore each other. The Sailor's Tavern had traders, travellers and all sorts coming in and out so new faces staying there for the night were nothing new. As the evening wore on, satisfied that Dobson's men had drunk themselves into a stupor and Ralph had fallen asleep drunk at a table; Daniel walked over to the lone man sitting with his ale, stumbling in a drunken manner to make conversation, but he wasn't drunk.

'Captain Munro, what in God's name are you doing here?' Daniel kept his voice low.

'I could ask you the same question, Daniel Sibson; let me buy you a drink?' Munro was calm.

'Aye, why not?' Daniel lifted his tankard getting the attention of the serving wench. Their tankards refilled they could talk without interruption.

'I'm pleased to see you and Ralph back home in Hastings, Sergeant Major, but I can see you've fallen in with the wrong crowd, a crowd that will end up getting you hung and poor

Ralph for that matter.' Munro angled his head at the pathetic figure of Ralph lying face down on a table in a drunken coma.

Munro's words startled Daniel. 'Talk like that in this place is dangerous, Captain. I doubt you came here to exchange pleasantries; what are you about here?'

'You were always good at getting to the point, Sergeant Major. I admit I never expected to see you and Ralph here, but, since you have found me, all I can tell you is that I am here on official business.'

'Captain, if any man here knew your history they'd stomp your head in before you could move a muscle. Drink your ale, finish your meal and leave now. There's a coach goes to London at midnight, get yourself on it and don't come back.' Daniel was doing his best to appear a calm drunk in conversation but in reality he was exasperated.

'Well, Daniel, if we are warning each other, then let me repay the compliment. Perhaps you can guess why I'm here in Hastings so this is your chance. Yes, I do know what you are about these days and that of your friends, it will be stopped, so believe me, this is your chance. Leave here and come to London, I'll get you sorted out with work. Ralph too; look at the state of him lying there, it's pathetic. I've helped other men from the regiment; come with me, Daniel.' For Munro to use Daniel's first name was proof that he was desperate to help his old Sergeant Major.

'Captain Munro, you know full well I respected you when we served together fighting Boney, but that's now history. I thank you for your concern, but no. Opening carriage doors for rich men in London won't cut it for me. This is and was always my home; at least here I have a fair crack of the whip, if you pardon the expression. You were always a good man; you did your duty and you're doing it now, and I still respect you for it.'

'As you wish, Sergeant Major and I respect you too; let me take Ralph at least?'

'I will take care of Ralph, Captain. In any case, his mind is set and he works with me. I wish you good luck even if the next time I meet you we are facing each other with weapons!'

'I wish you good luck as well, Sergeant Major.' Munro finished his tankard of ale and stood up, shook hands with Daniel and then walked out of the Sailor's, leaving Daniel sitting at the table.

Smith walked over to the table swaying and bumping into other drinkers before falling into an empty chair opposite Daniel.

'Who was that?' he slurred.

'Just some trader from London I was trying to get on our side, he wasn't interested,' Daniel shrugged his shoulders and drunk from his tankard as he lied. As Smith went back to drink more with the rest of the gang Daniel's heart was thumping so much, perhaps Ralph was right and all this would end badly. Standing up Ralph he dragged his old friend out of the Sailor's Tavern and walked him back home, he'd lost his interest in drinking this night.

Chapter Four
The Great Fight

Daniel should have been happy but in his heart he was anything but. Munro had given him a warning and he was incapable of doing anything about it. Should he up sticks with Ralph and leave Hastings or warn Dobson and hope his brutal master wouldn't murder him, thinking he was a traitor? At the same time, he was in denial; driving Miss Laura every day hoping nothing would change but he was too experienced to know that in life nothing stays the same. The orphanage in Bexhill was the one thing that put a smile on Daniel's face; where previously he carried the bread basket for Miss Laura, he now helped her to give out the rolls to the children. To his own surprise he had enjoyed being with the children, they climbed on his back and they hung off his arms and legs, he would walk with his new found friends like a human Christmas tree. All the children would laugh, as did Laura, it pleased her to see Daniel happy in sharing kindness with the orphans. Then there was little Maria, Daniel would always spend some minutes talking to her. As it happened, Daniel said very few words, Maria would talk away about flowers, playing, anything and Daniel would just listen. The child knew nothing but how to be kind and enjoy her life, difficult as it was; if only others could appreciate how lucky they were, he would think.

The visit to the orphanage would always happen on a Wednesday and Daniel forgot the ills on his mind looking forward to seeing the children, especially the little girl he had protected on his first visit.

On this Wednesday morning, as Miss Laura got into the carriage, she noticed the smile on Daniel's face.

'Good morning, Daniel, you appear very content this day?'

'Good morning to you, Miss Laura. Yes, I am happy, I enjoy visiting the orphanage,' Daniel answered.

'That pleases me very much to hear that, Daniel. Shall we away there?'

Miss Laura was happy and so was Daniel and off they went to Bexhill on a fine morning, things couldn't be better.

They had been on the road for a quarter of an hour when a lone horseman riding in the opposite direction pulled his mount to a stop and raised his hand in recognition of Laura. The rider was dressed finely as would be expected of any country gentleman.

'Good morning, Miss Laura,' the rider greeted.

'Good morning to you, Sir John, I trust you are well?' she answered politely as would be expected of any well-educated young lady.

'I'm well, Miss Laura, and where are you off to this fine morning?' Sir John asked while patting his horse.

'To visit the children at the orphanage in Bexhill,' Laura answered.

Sir John acknowledged Laura's answer, then turned his attention to Daniel. 'What regiment?'

Daniel was taken by surprise.

'Sir?' he stuttered.

'I said, what regiment, man; who did you serve with in the war?' Sir John asked again.

'35th, sir, the Sussex Regiment,' Daniel answered, hesitant of what the next question would be.

'Ah, the Sussex Regiment. What a square you made at Waterloo! Judging by the burns on your face, you served a long time. Your name?' Sir John continued his interrogation.

'Sibson, Sergeant Major Daniel Sibson.' Daniel waited for the reaction.

'Sergeant Major, a shame you didn't come to me first I could have found you honest work,' Sir John said glancing at Laura.

Daniel had had enough. 'Honest work? I looked everywhere, had too many doors slammed in my face, so don't sit there on your fine horse sneering at me about my work.'

Sir John, taken aback by Daniel's answer, regretted his tone and turned back to Laura.

'I thank you for your work with the orphans, Miss Laura. I only wish your father could use his talents as you do. I bid you good day.' Sir John touched the rim of his hat and with the flick of the reins was on his way.

Daniel followed suit, tapping the horses lightly with the riding whip and the carriage was on its way again too.

'May I ask you who that was, Miss Laura?' Daniel asked.

'That was Sir John Rutherford, the local magistrate. How did he know you were in the army?' Laura was curious.

'A Brown Bess musket has a sharp flame that comes up out of the priming pan when you pull the trigger; it catches the right side of your face a bit. When you fire a Brown Bess so many times over the years, you end up with the redness I and all the other veterans have on our cheek,' Daniel said.

'I see,' Laura said and contented herself with her newfound knowledge.

Daniel meanwhile grinded his teeth. First meeting Munro and now the local magistrate; this didn't auger well.

They arrived at the orphanage without any further meetings on the road. While Laura walked inside the main hall to speak with the governess, Daniel secured the reins of the carriage horse then picking up the large basket of bread rolls followed Laura inside. Just like every visit, the children sat on the floor eagerly waiting for their weekly treat, but something was wrong; he could see it on Laura's face as she spoke with the governess.

Laura turned to face Daniel; she was worried and nervous. 'Daniel, it would be best if you leave the basket here and wait for me outside. I shan't be long.'

'What is it, Miss Laura, what's wrong?'

Before Laura could answer, Daniel turned and starting looking for his little friend Maria amidst the faces of the children. He walked around the hall, looking for her, but she wasn't there! He felt a hand on his shoulder; he knew it was Laura but didn't want to turn around.

'Daniel, I have just talked to the governess. I fear I have bad news to tell you. Your little friend Maria took to coughing last week and it got worse. She just wasn't strong enough; I'm afraid she passed away yesterday.' Laura could feel herself biting her lip as she uttered the words, watching Daniel as he turned to face her.

'Miss Laura, just find out for me where she is buried.' Daniel's face was ashen, he then strode out of the hall.

Some minutes later near an apple orchard in the orphanage grounds Daniel and Laura stood over the mound of soil with a wooden crucifix driven into it that was Maria's grave. Daniel had picked some nearby flowers and laid them on top of the grave; then he sunk down onto his knees dropping his face into his hands and did something he hadn't done in years, he wept.

Standing behind Daniel, Laura could do little but put her hand on his shoulder as tears rolled down her cheeks.

'Daniel, we can do no more. We should leave little Maria in peace with our prayers.' She put her hand under his arm and motioned for Daniel to stand up which he did, but his sadness had turned to anger.

'No, Miss Laura, you're wrong; there's much more we can do. Look at her grave, not even a headstone! What sort of people are we? I spent years killing Frenchmen I didn't even know, but I can't protect a girl of five from dying in poverty! Damn this world, damn this place... I... I'm sorry!' Daniel stormed away and sat back in the carriage.

Laura left Daniel to it and went back into the hall to give some sustenance to the children inside.

Daniel had recomposed himself by the time Laura rejoined him in the carriage. 'Miss Laura, I am sorry for my outburst. I—'

But Laura cut him off.

'Daniel, you have shown me today, and at other times, for that matter, that you are a man of great compassion. I assure you there is no need to be sorry.' As Laura said this she held his hand and for a brief moment she and Daniel just looked into each other's eyes and souls.

'You were right before, Miss Laura, this is no life for me working for your father. I can do better things.'

'Then I urge you, Daniel, take your friend and leave Hastings now. There is a new world for you in America or somewhere else. Go now before things go bad.' Laura was still holding his hand.

'I would go now but there is something holding me here.'

'What could be keeping you here? Go now, Daniel, while you still can.'

'You, you are the reason I'll stay and I won't go anywhere until I know you are safe.'

Laura went to answer, but Daniel released her hand and put his hand on her face. 'I couldn't protect little Maria, but I can and will protect you, Laura. So there it is. Where are we off to now?'

Feeling the heat on her face as it turned red, Laura stammered and then found the words she needed.

'It has been a difficult morning, Daniel, perhaps you should take me back home.'

The carriage drove away back to Battle carrying two people who didn't speak because, in their own way, they knew they were falling in love.

'The fact is, Captain, they knew we were coming.' Tinsley's voice was shaking as he said it, his hand gripped tightly around a mug of rum.

'Go on, Tinsley.' Captain Townsend wanted to hear more and patiently took his time as he debriefed Tinsley, pacing around the room on the top floor of the Martello Tower. Gazing out of the musket slit towards the sea, Townsend gave the impression he wasn't listening but he was taking in every word Tinsley was saying.

'When we got to the top of the hill, they were lined up and ready, fired a volley and then flew into us, we didn't stand a chance.'

'You weren't there by chance though, Sergeant. How was the operation instigated?'

Tinsley's head lifted up; he looked even more nervous. Sensing this, Townsend reassured the sergeant.

'Sergeant Tinsley, I know you are a good man. I'm here to find the rogues that killed your comrades, you are not under suspicion but as the only survivor from the West Hill your testimony is important. Will you help me?'

'Of course, sir. Well, it was the town constable.'

Townsend stopped walking and stood still he looked directly at Tinsley.

'What about the town constable?' The questioning was getting somewhere.

'A man called Tappin; he came to see Captain Hardwicke that morning here at the tower. It was after Tappin left that Captain Hardwicke got all excited and had us go up the West Hill the same evening.'

Townsend then asked a leading question. 'Did the town constable meet you the evening that you were attacked on the West Hill?'

'No sir, he was nowhere to be seen.'

In a few minutes Townsend had found enough to begin his first operation.

'That will be all for now, Sergeant. Now I have a deal to make with you.'

'Yes, sir,' Tinsley answered in some anticipation.

'For my part, I swear I will bring to justice the men who attacked you. In exchange, I want you to show me that you can lead the men downstairs, can you do this?'

'Yes, sir, I can.' Tinsley had a smile on his face.

'Good. Then let's get to work.'

As Tinsley saluted and left the office Townsend decided it was time to get acquainted with Mister Tappin, the town constable.

It was a busy evening as ever in the Sailor's Tavern and Dobson was in a good mood; all his cronies were gathered around him and the ale was flowing. Certain that the tavern was packed to the gills so he could speak in confidence, Dobson in his usual fashion whispered into Watson's ear. Watson gathered the main men together – among them Smith, Harrison, Daniel and Ralph – and ushered them to a table that would accommodate them.

'So, some of you may have heard that there is a bare-knuckle prize-fight happening in London in two days' time… on Blackheath, to be precise. A fight that will decide the championship of the world. Between our own man, Tom Cribb, and the freed American slave, Tom Molineaux. They fought a hard bout before and Cribb won it, just! This one is the decider and I have a lot of money on this fight.'

Confident that he had the complete interest of his men Dobson continued.

'As you know, I enjoy prize-fighting, you know full well my man Harrison is my finest boxer and one day I will have him beating Cribb. So, here's the thing, Watson you will keep an eye on things here for me. Smith, you'll stay here with Watson, and Harrison, you're with me. Sibson, you will follow us with my daughter and you may bring your friend if you wish.' He nodded at Ralph; this brought some raised eyebrows from the rest of the group.

'One more thing lads, I may be going to Blackheath to see the greatest fight that will ever happen on these shores but I also have business to attend to. There will be people there that I must speak with and, if it goes well for me, so it will be for you as well.'

'Have no fears, Mister Dobson, I'll look after things fine while you're away,' Watson chipped in, smiling.

Daniel said nothing as he detested crawling but at the same time was no more proud of himself as he was taking money from the same person.

'You better had,' Dobson growled banging his tankard on the table making everyone jump, most of all Watson. Intimidation was Dobson's way of asserting power; satisfied he had done this, Dobson nodded to Harrison and both men walked out of the Sailor's.

Feeling safe again, Watson, Smith and the rest of the group broke away to carry on drinking. As Daniel downed a tankard, Ralph stared at this friend.

'You're not right, Daniel, and you haven't been for some time. What irks you, Sergeant Major?'

Daniel laughed at the use of his army title. 'I have a fear, Ralph; when you first told me this thing would end badly, perhaps you had reason.'

'Why would you say such a thing, Daniel? What is wrong with you?'

'I don't know, Ralph. Just stay close to me, whatever happens, and let's get an early night before our trip to London.'

Walking back to their lodgings both men were silent but Daniel's brain was thumping. The little girl's death, the warning from Munro and his growing feelings for Laura... how would this all end?

Watson had stayed on in the Sailor's to keep drinking, he was feeling smug because Dobson would be away for a few days and he would be in charge of things. Like the rest of the gang he failed to recognise that the greatest enemy the smugglers had was that of arrogance. Arrogance to the point of stupidity; where they were so confident after the fight on the West Hill that they felt untouchable. Walking outside to urinate against a wall; he was drunk and careless having no idea he was being watched by two men standing in a darkened doorway a few yards away.

'Do we take him now, sir?' one of the watchers asked.

'No, let them all drink themselves into extinction, if we have to wait all night so be it but he's the one we want,' answered Munro pulling his overcoat collar up around his neck to keep warm.

The smugglers may have thought of themselves as modern day Robin Hoods but they were hated because the ordinary people tolerated them out of fear and no other reason.

They were thugs who had plenty of enemies in the town and, for Munro, getting information was not difficult.

It was after midnight when Watson staggered down the main street singing a dirge to himself. He was conscious of a figure walking towards him who wouldn't move out of his way but he was so drunk he was seeing double.

'Get out of my way, don't you know who I am?' He shouted.

The figure stayed still, then there was movement and he felt a blow on his head. For Watson, everything went black.

There was a feeling of being shaken then Watson heard words but couldn't see anything, a bag or something was over his head he could feel the material move as he breathed against it, his head was throbbing and he felt sick from drinking too much ale. He was sitting down and tried to stand up but was unable to as his hands were tied around the back of the chair and he couldn't move.

'Wake up, you piece of scum!' He was being shouted at. Next the hood was pulled off his head and he blinked from the light; several men he didn't recognise were standing over him.

'Who are you, how do you know my name, what do you want?' Watson was blabbering.

'We're asking the questions, Watson. Tell us about you and your smuggling mates.' One of the men leaned close to his face.

'Smuggling, what would I know about that? I'm just a fisherman.' Watson was too scared to be a convincing liar.

The interrogator stood back from Watson and laughed. Watson's eyes started to adjust better to the light and he looked around the room. No windows, just candles providing light and a single door; as for his captors, they were wearing the unmistakable red tunics of the British Army.

'The army, what's the army got to do with me?' Watson asked his interrogator.

Ignoring Watson, Captain Munro turned to the nearest soldier. 'Sergeant, I think our friend Watson needs some encouragement. Best you encourage him.'

'Very good, sir.'

The sergeant walked behind Watson, then he felt a piece of material that smelt like leather being wrapped tight around his throat. He started to gag, he couldn't breathe. Munro leaned into Watson's face again, so close he could smell his breath.

'It's simple, Watson; you will tell us everything you know on the smuggling operation or we keep tightening that piece of leather until you pass out, then we do it again.'

Watson was choking, the strip of leather around his neck was tightened, then it was released, he could breathe again, his throat was throbbing, he coughed and sat up, then a punch hit him in the stomach, he bent over double and fell sideways onto the floor.

'Get him back on his feet.' The chair and Watson were manhandled back up straight again.

'Well, Watson, now you know we can choke you, punch you and eventually we'll kill you.'

'Kill me? You can't, you're the law!' Watson in his pain and confusion became defiant.

'Ah Watson, that is true, we are the law, but we have orders from on high to finish your little gang once and for all and that means using any means at our disposal. You must understand everything has changed, you had it so good for a long time, but now we can use whatever is necessary to finish your little enterprise so let's start again. I want to know everything about your operation.'

'Then strangle me, kill me if you must; but I'm not speaking cos my boss will kill me if he finds out I talked to you!'

'As you wish, Watson, but before we do that you might want to say goodbye to someone.'

Munro nodded to the other soldier; he opened the door and a woman and child were manhandled into the room by two men.

'Jack, what are they doing to us?' pleaded the woman in tears. The child was a little girl, no older than ten; she was struggling and being held away as she tried to reach out to her mother.

Watson tried to jump out of the chair, but was held back in by his captors. 'You blackguards, what are you doing with my wife and child?' Watson didn't realise it, but tears were streaming down his face.

'Well, Watson, killing is easy; I saw lots of it fighting Napoleon. Men, women, children, they died in their thousands so another dead woman and child makes no difference to me.' Munro turned to the two men and the sergeant. 'Sergeant, take them both outside as I'm getting bored, put your bayonet to them. The child first, I want the mother to watch her die.'

Watson screamed, 'No, no, leave them be! I'll tell you everything!'

'Well, Watson, here's the deal. You will stop wasting my time and tell me everything you know. If I believe you they live, if I think you are lying, they both die, now start talking!'

'Please, no, sir, I can tell you now Dobson is going away soon to watch the Cribb fight in London, there's much more, just please don't hurt my family.'

'London, eh? I've heard about this bout between Cribb and Molineaux, our friend Dobson is very ambitious, I'm sure you have lots more to tell us.'

Watson couldn't speak any more, he just nodded his head in compliance.

Leaving Watson to stew he nodded at the men with Watson's family who dragged them out of the room. Going outside with the sergeant Munro was confident he had Watson where he wanted him.

'Right, take your time with him, Sergeant; I don't care how long it takes. Release his binds, give him food and drink; I want him lucid as we get our information from him, while he's worried about his family he'll tell us all.'

'How long will we keep him, sir?'

'That man is going nowhere sergeant. Find out where he lives and make it look as though he and the family have made a run for it. Get some men and break into that building they have in town, take money if you can find it and a few other things, I want this Dobson character to start feeling somewhat nervous.'

'What about the family, sir?' the sergeant asked expectantly.

'Oh yes, I nearly forgot my little bluff worked. They will stay here for the time being; ensure they have everything they need to be comfortable but they can't leave. If Watson behaves, we might even let them see him.'

'Sir.'

As the sergeant answered, Munro was already striding away, his mind was already thinking about what he would do once they had squeezed Watson for everything he had. Munro was also thinking about his journey to London; he was also going to watch the great fight.

Blackheath was the perfect location for the rematch between Cribb and Molineaux. The park had plenty of rolling heathland where the ring for the fight could be set up; not to mention space for the thousands of people who had come to watch. It wasn't just about the fight; south London was making a day of the event. Countless tents and pavilions had been erected for the day where alcohol, food and other delights were on sale. Thousands of guineas were riding on this bout so amongst the keen pugilists were men gambling their last few shillings, milling around with families having picnics on the heath who were curious about the day's events. Probably fifteen thousand people were present on Blackheath this day making the atmosphere charged and exciting. Walking through the crowds and exploring the different wares of the various merchants who had set up shop for the day was Laura chaperoned by Daniel and Ralph. Laura was resplendent, dressed in a countryside lady's dress, wearing a bonnet and carrying a summer parasol that she twirled around as she walked, attracting the attention of many a gentleman's eye. As for Daniel and Ralph, they looked like what they were; tidily dressed thugs with a job to safely escort the pretty young lady.

'What do you think, Daniel?' Laura had a habit of initiating conversations with an open question.

'What I think, Miss Laura, is that we should enjoy this part of the day; as for the rest, I'm not sure.' It was going to be one of those discussions that they had from time to time.

'Oh, why so, Daniel? What could be wrong with two men lawfully bettering themselves in the only way available to them with their wits and their muscles? What do you think, Ralph?'

'I think your argument is reasonable, Miss Laura, but you may change your mind after you watch the first round.' He smiled in a knowing way as he said this.

'My oh my, you two are both very miserable today, but I won't let you spoil my day in London. Now let's look in here.' Off walked Laura into a marquee selling goods for fashionable ladies. The two veteran soldiers looked at each other with eyes raised and followed her inside.

While Laura was enjoying the day her father had business to attend to. Many of the tents set up on Blackheath had been hired for the day by individuals or groups as their own hostelry where they could meet up, drink ale and talk business, rubbish or whatever. Outside one such tent stood Harrison, silent, tall and as intimidating as ever but he was not alone. There were several other men of a similar appearance and character standing with Harrison: their job was to ensure that their bosses, drinking ale inside the tent, were not disturbed. Inside the tent, as well as the drinking, a battle of egos and boasting was taking place. Dobson was there from Sussex but there were also leaders of smuggling gangs who came from all over the south coast in Kent and Hampshire. They were men who were brazen, they felt invincible and now they were all getting together.

Dobson looked around the group as they drunk and talked and decided it was the right moment to start the meeting; he started to bang his metal tankard on the wooden table he sat at until there was silence.

'I am pleased you are here to enjoy the bout, gentlemen, and it should be a good day depending on where you wager your purse.' He emphasised the last few words, getting some guffaws.

'First let us talk business, gentlemen, and then we can watch the fight.'

There were many strong personalities in the tent, among them a man called Tibbs. Tibbs headed up a gang running out of Dover, he was equally as ruthless as Dobson.

'Then let's talk business, Dobson; what do you have in mind?' Tibbs asked with a sarcastic expression on his face.

'An alliance, gentlemen. We're strong in our own gangs – what if we were to work together?'

'What's in it for me and the rest of us if we work together?' Dobson had Tibbs' attention and that of the others.

'You know my gang had a run in with the Duty Men a few weeks ago and we bloodied their noses for them,' Dobson was about to go on but was interrupted.

'Your gang is not the first to kill a few Duty Men,' another smuggler butted in.

Sensing the pessimism amongst the group Dobson knew he had to roll with the punches.

'I'm sure that's true, but the point I was going to make was that we can kill them but more will come back, stronger and better organised and then there's us squabbling between ourselves for whatever we can get.'

Tibbs seemed to become the spokesman for the group and piped up again.

'So what do you suggest, Dobson?'

'It's simple; there's enough cream to go around, gentlemen. Instead of fighting between ourselves over loads coming from France; where it's on the edge of our territories we take turns on who gets it. We can keep having tear ups amongst our gangs or we deal properly with the Duty Men.' Like any good speaker, Dobson waited for his words to sink in and take effect.

There was murmuring and whispering to each other in the group.

'Carry on, Dobson.' Tibbs had become curious as well.

'I don't know about you, but I have no intention to change my trade; I'm in this until the death. What I suggest is that, where we know "His Majesty's Preventative Service" are planning something, we stretch them as thin as possible – they can't be everywhere at once. If they think something is happening in Hastings then we feed them information that something is going on elsewhere. We want them running round like headless chickens and, in the meantime, we keep collecting our contraband with no interference. When they do get too close, then we bloody their noses so much they won't ever come back. I'm not asking none of you to give up nothing just we use our brains if we're gonna keep going as we are.' Dobson tapped his temple with his finger as he said this and looked to each man he was addressing. Heads were nodding and there was more murmuring.

'So what next, Dobson?' someone asked.

'There is no "next" just now, I don't expect any of you to say yes or no today. For now, we drink some more ale, talk between ourselves and then we meet again in a few weeks to see how we work this.'

Dobson, thinking he had the other leaders on his side, sat down. More ale was served and for the next hour they talked excitedly between each other about Dobson's proposition and who would win the fight. One man drank slowly and kept his own counsel, Tibbs, he stared long and hard at Dobson as he walked around the tent working his influence on the other gang leaders as they got drunk. The time for the prize-fight was getting closer; Dobson took out his timepiece from his waistcoat and, after eyeing it, stood up.

'Well, gentlemen, we have a fight to watch; shall we?'

They drained the final dregs of ale in their tankards, shook hands and stumbled outside to be escorted to the bout by their muscled minders led by Dobson and Harrison. One person remained behind, Tibbs, who walked around the back of the tent on the pretense of emptying his bladder. Tibbs waited a few minutes until he was joined by a tall distinguished looking man wearing a long riding coat and the typical attire of a country gentleman.

'Let's not pretend we are friends, Tibbs; tell me what's gone on inside that tent and you get your money.'

'Now, now, why so hostile? This is a business transaction; I've been paying Duty Men money for years, so it makes a change for them to pay me something.' Tibbs was a born rogue and enjoyed making anyone in authority uncomfortable.

'If this is business, as you say, then get on with it and you get your money.'

'Fair enough.' Over the next few minutes Tibbs went on to recount everything that was discussed between the leaders of the smuggling gangs, as he finished talking he held his hand out.

'So much for honour amongst thieves,' said the man as he dropped a large canvas purse full of coins into Tibbs' hand.

'There was never such a thing. You just stay away from me and my gang, and I'll keep feeding you information on Dobson, but remember: you need to give me more of this.' Tibbs shook the bag of coins in his hand.

'There will be more coin for you, Tibbs, but you will have to do things for me.'

'I'm listening.' Tibbs was interested.

'I will let you know when, but I want one of your runners to take a message to Dobson about a shipment of wine and tobacco that will be arriving in Rye harbor. That's all you need to do.'

'Normally, I would keep a job like that to myself – why should Dobson believe me?'

'Well, you're all good friends now. Convince him it's a favour and in any case you have a job in Dover and can't spare the men for it.'

'As you wish, soldier boy.' Tibbs laughed as the last words came out of his mouth.

With lightning speed, Munro grabbed the front of Tibbs' jacket and pulled him close so both faces were almost touching. Tibbs was caught completely off-guard and off-balance. He was startled; the thug wasn't used to being bullied.

'Listen to me you piece of scum, don't think because I'm wearing a fine suit that I'm a nice person. If you ever use those words to me again I'll smash your face in so much that you'll be even uglier than you already are, now get lost!' Munro pushed Tibbs away so violently that he staggered backwards almost falling over. Tibbs rearranged his jacket and stared at Munro as he walked away hoping no one had seen him being manhandled, this wouldn't be good for his reputation. Captain Munro stayed back behind the tent to think on the conversation with Tibbs. Smugglers working as a coalition, more attacks on the Preventative Service, these were dangerous ideas but he wouldn't let it get that far. As for Tibbs, was he too stupid to realise that, once the Hastings gang were dealt with, he and his gang of thugs would be next?

It was a fine, sunny afternoon in south London as the two most famous boxers in the world climbed through the ropes into the ring on the field of Blackheath. The ring was raised up eight feet above the watching crowd, this way it was possible to stand just about anywhere and watch the fight with an unobstructed view. The ring surface was constructed of wooden planks and roped off on the edges to keep both fighters confined and away from the crowd. This was done with good reason; in their first meeting the spectators had invaded the fighting space and attacked Molineaux. Although the decision of the bout had been given to Cribb, the ring invasion and other incidents in the fight had made the result controversial, thus the bout this day in Blackheath would be the decider. Dobson had used Harrison as a battering ram to push his way to the front of the crowd and get a ringside position. Laura, Daniel and Ralph had followed in Harrison's wake and stood behind Dobson. The atmosphere at the fight was like nothing Daniel had ever experienced in his life. Over fifteen thousand people were jam-packed together and waiting in anticipation for the pugilists to arrive. A murmuring in the crowd changed to cheering and as Daniel looked to his left; there was movement as the people there pushed back to make a space. Then they appeared, climbing through the ropes into the ring with their trainers. First to enter the ring was Tom Cribb and then Tom Molineaux followed behind him, both of them bare-chested. It was rumoured that Cribb had lost a stone in weight since the first bout and to be sure he looked fit, muscular and strong. As for Molineaux, he was the finest specimen of a human being Daniel had ever seen, muscled all over and in superb condition. While the boxers stretched and warmed up speaking with their trainers, a group of men who were the fight officials stood talking in a group in the centre of the ring. As for Daniel and Laura, they couldn't help themselves and became more excited as one man amongst those standing in the ring started proceedings. His first words were drowned out by the noise of the spectators until they realised what was happening.

'Ladies and Gentlemen, we are here to decide upon the prize-fighting championship of the world. On my left, all the way from Virginia, America, the man called the Black Ajax, Mister Tom Molineaux.' Molineaux's trainer raised his fighter's arm, but there were no cheers, just boos and insults. Molineaux, however, heard nothing and stared hard to the other side of the ring at Cribb.

The announcer continued, 'On my right, from Bristol, our own British Champion; Mister Tom Cribb.'

The crowd howled and cheered for Cribb and, if anything, Cribb's muscled chest grew bigger as the noise carried on.

'The bout will continue until one boxer is knocked out or is unable to defend himself; fighters, go back to your corners.'

The bell rang starting the fight and more cheers came from the crowd, Cribb and Molineaux moved towards and then around each other arms raised covering their chests and faces in the classic pugilist stance. The crowds were waiting in anticipation for the first blows to be struck. Laura could feel herself holding her breath and then she shrieked in horror. In her sheltered life, she had never witnessed real violence, but now it was in front of her. Cribb threw the first punch that caught Molineaux flush on the chin; Molineaux was stunned but shook his head and walked forward into more punches from Cribb, taking punishment so that he could close on his opponent. The noise of Cribb's punches connecting with the head of Molineux was horrible and as each blow was struck Laura stopped screaming and winced holding her hand over her mouth. Daniel saw the distress of Laura, but decided, for the time being, to leave her be.

How the two men set about each other. It was obvious that Cribb was an experienced boxer who knew how to use the complete space of the ring. Without any doubt Molineaux was the stronger man and any time his punches landed Cribb was hurt. Cribb tried to ride his opponent's punches pulling his head back; he knew for himself from the first bout that Molineaux was stronger than him, so his tactic was to box not fight and take less punishment. Molineaux kept walking into punches to get close to Cribb, but, as the rounds passed, the punishment he was enduring took effect and he started to tire. Each bonecracking punch that Cribb and Molineaux hit each other with made Daniel flinch; Ralph couldn't bear to watch and turned around, pushing his way back through the crowd to get away. Dobson was completely the opposite, oblivious to the discomfort of his daughter he clapped his hands and hooted with delight every time Cribb got a good punch in. Daniel was aware that Ralph had gone then he felt a hand grab his own hand, it was Laura, she squeezed his hand all the time but kept facing the ring with tears running down her face. For round after round, Cribb tried to avoid the sledgehammers being thrown by Molineaux; while the American kept getting picked off by the defensive boxing of Cribb.

It was the eleventh round and both boxers had taken too much punishment. Their faces were battered and bloody but of the two men Molineux looked the worse for wear and was exhausted having borne more blows. Whilst the two boxers may have been tired the watching crowds were the complete opposite, they were frenzied and cheered more awaiting the next round. As both fighters got up from their stools Molineaux was almost stumbling. Approaching Cribb his guard was low and one of his eyes was so swollen his head was at an awkward angle trying to get a look at Cribb from his good eye. Molineaux threw a tired hook that Cribb easily side-stepped; Cribb then stepped inside and hit Molineaux full on the left side of his face with an almighty thump sending him up and then falling flat on his back on the ring floor. There was a horrible crack; anyone close enough to hear the sound recoiled in the horror of it, Molineaux's jaw was broken! Molineaux's face, already bloody and swollen, blew up like a cow's udder, it was an awful sight. Dobson laughed and cheered as did many of the watching spectators. Daniel felt his heart sink, two great men in their prime, he couldn't bear to watch them damage each other in such a manner. He had seen so much blood and agony when he served in Wellington's army but this was akin to watching a slow torture. Laura kept hold of Daniel's hand and said nothing, what could she say? As for Harrison the pugilist, his reaction was interesting: no shouting or cheering, just a shake of his head as Molineaux tried to get back up on his feet.

Molineaux bravely stood up and tried to fight but he disappeared under a flurry of punches from Cribb who closed in on him like a hunter after a kill. Molineaux was on the floor again on all floors with Cribb standing over him waiting for him to get up. There were shouts from Molineaux's corner and the referee waved his arms crossing them in an "over" motion and then raised Cribb's arm in the air. That was it, Cribb had won! Molineaux's trainers walked him backed to his corner where he collapsed onto his stool. Molineaux was completely broken; this wonderful man who had fought so hard all his life to get to this place could not fight any more, it was an awful sight. As for Cribb, he stood up, realising the fight was won and then leaned forward in relief, exhausted, his hands on his knees. Within a moment, the crowd had mobbed the fighting space and he was hoisted up on the shoulders of his followers. He was now jubilant, as he should have been. Molineaux was a fighting machine, but Cribb had bested him and he was the best in the world. As Daniel saw Molineaux slumped on his stool with his jaw swollen to three times its normal size, he thought how much he hated the human race. How could any people, who claimed to be civilised, enjoy watching two human beings beat each other to a pulp and, in the case of

Molineaux, almost to death? He thought it a disgusting spectacle.

Dobson however was delighted. Turning around he kissed and hugged his daughter, having no concern for her distressed appearance. He was doubly pleased with the way the meeting had gone with the other gang leaders and he had bet twenty guineas on Cribb and won. To his mind everything was going his way.

'I'm staying here a while, Laura; I have more entertaining to do. Sibson here will take you back to Hastings. Travel safe now and I'll see you at home in a day or so.'

'Yes, father,' Laura answered obediently and watched her father walk away with Harrison to get even closer to the celebrations in the ring.

'Shall we go, Miss Laura?' Daniel asked meekly.

'Please, Daniel; let us leave this place as soon as possible. I never want to remember what I have seen here this day.'

Laura took hold of Daniel's arm and then they moved through the crowd away from the ring intending to find Ralph and their carriage to travel home.

It was a blustery morning in Hastings and Tappin stood outside the Custom House. He was enjoying the view of the sea that lay across the other side of the cobbled road that ran the length of the seafront. Since the massacre on the West Hill he had been in a deep depression because he knew that, although he hadn't fired a shot, it was he who had condemned the Duty Men to death. Gazing at the sea calmed him down but he had become withdrawn. In his heart he knew that turning a blind eye to smugglers dealing in contraband goods was one thing but being an accomplice to murder was a different story. Tappin was religious in his own way and believed that he would pay for his sins in the end. It was in this quiet moment of self-pity that he noticed several men in blue uniform tunics walking towards him from the direction of the town. As the men got closer he could see one was dressed in a Royal Navy officer's uniform, the other two looked like Duty Men. All three men were walking with a purpose. Tappin became nervous, they were striding toward him and he started to stagger back to the main entrance door. Then they were on him, the officer stood and stared at Tappin then nodded his head at the two Duty Men with him. They picked up Tappin and lifted his feet off the floor into the Custom House, then threw him over the table in the front office. Tappin landed in a dazed, confused heap. The officer followed inside and closed the entrance door behind him. Tappin stayed huddled on the floor not knowing what to expect next. The officer paced around the front office pretending to inspect it then he turned and walked to Tappin and leaned down over him.

'Are you the town constable, Tappin?'

'Yes, sir, I am,' Tappin answered hopefully, but his hopes were dashed as the officer grabbed him close by the lapels of his jacket and pulled his face close.

'No, you are not the town constable! You are a corrupt, treacherous, little man! Did you really think you could lead ten officers of His Majesty's Preventative Service to a trap where they were all killed and get away with it?'

That was it, no more questions were necessary. Tappin pulled away and, rolling himself into a foetal position on the floor, started crying like a child, moaning repeatedly, 'I'm sorry, I'm sorry, God forgive me.'

Townsend and the two Duty Men were experienced at this and left him to cry. After a few minutes, they got him up and sat him back at the table with a mug of rum in his hand to fortify his spirit. After breaking their man, now was the time to build him up again. After ten minutes and a few sips of rum, Tappin had calmed down.

'What will you do with me, Captain?'

'It's all about cooperation, Tappin. I want the truth from you about the West Hill. If I think for a moment you're lying, then you'll swing from a rope; the choice is yours.'

'Where should I start?' Tappin looked to the faces of the three men standing over him.

'At the beginning, Tappin, we have plenty of time.'

For the next two hours Tappin sang like a canary telling Townsend everything, including his collusion in the massacre on the West Hill. After Captain Townsend was satisfied he had squeezed Tappin for everything he knew. The three men got up to leave the Custom House and Tappin was flabbergasted.

'Is that it, is nothing else happening to me?'

Townsend laughed. 'Don't be stupid, Tappin, you belong to me now. Keep playing along with Dobson as usual, but my men will be back to see you often and you will tell them everything your paymaster does, we may even need you to pass some news back to him. I warn you not to get any foolish ideas or you will get the rope.'

Outside, Townsend turned to one of the Duty Men a faint smile on his face. 'Does that feel better, Sergeant Tinsley?'

'Much better, thank you, sir,' Tinsley answered.

'Good. That fool doesn't know it, but he'll be a vital part of our first action against those thugs.'

Tinsley strode after Captain Townsend with a purpose.

After his attackers had left, Tappin stayed sat at the table where they left him. He drained the last of the rum in his mug, then, with a trembling hand, he refilled the mug and started to down more rum; he knew he was doomed whatever he did.

The journey back from London was a quiet one; there was no conversation between the three travellers. Laura sat in the back of the carriage and did her best to read from a book despite the bumpy road. Daniel and Ralph were driving and riding in the front, leaving Laura in peace. Two experienced men, they could read the sadness etched on her face since they left the ring at Blackheath. The countryside in Kent was beautiful and made a pleasant contrast from the noise of the baying mobs and the sheer brutality they had experienced in London. The carriage made its way along the windy road through the green fields, then Laura put her book away and the more she gazed, the more a smile came to her face. After an overnight stay at a coach house in the spa town of Royal Tunbridge Wells, they arrived back at Dobson's house in Battle by lunchtime of the next day. Almost as soon as they arrived Laura had gone into the house to change and refresh herself before eating. Daniel and Ralph took the horses to the stables to look after them. Taking the heavy leather straps off, they rubbed the horses down giving them fresh hay, water and fodder. Their work done, Daniel and Ralph sat down outside the stables and ate a lunch of hot sliced beef, cheese and bread washed down with a tankard of ale that a maid from the house brought out to them.

After a long journey and hard work, the lunch was well received.

'Still quiet, Daniel, what's going through your mind?' Ralph could read his friends mind easily.

'It was the bout, you had the sense to walk away early but when I saw Molineaux sitting on his stool I thought of the dead Duty Men lying up there on the West Hill and to think I killed one of them.'

'I don't judge you, Daniel. While you fired your musket that night, I was loading contraband crates in the caves; we were both doing something wrong in the wrong place. More to the point, Sergeant Major, do we sit here grinding our teeth making ourselves mad or do we get out of it?'

'You've answered the question for us, Ralph; we get out of here and find something else to do. I thought we had finished with violence in the army, but here we are, home in Hastings, and nothing has changed. My hands and my eyes are bloodied and I'm sick of it.' Daniel turned to look directly at his friend as he said this.

'Good, when do we leave?' Ralph was keen.

'Maybe it's time for a real change, Ralph; there's nothing here for us any more. Let's gather any coins we have and pay our way to America, I'm told if you work hard there's land aplenty for the taking and we start a new life there and maybe even find us some wives!'

For the first time in days they both laughed and did so heartily.

'Right, I'll get fresh horses and you prepare the carriage we can get back to our lodgings and start counting our coins,'

Ralph was up and gone while Daniel went back into the stables.

Having chosen the horses he would use, Daniel was fitting a bridle on one of them while patting and rubbing the horse's magnificently muscled neck. There was a feeling, as the hairs on the back of his neck stood up, that someone was watching him. Daniel turned back to look at the stable door and, leaning against the door frame with her head leaning sideways, touching the wood, was Laura. Daniel had always thought Laura beautiful but at this moment he had trouble to catch his breath. Laura had changed from the stuffy formal dress she had to wear when in public to a flowing summer frock with a flower decoration on it, she wore no bonnet and her long auburn hair was hanging loose over her shoulders.

'Miss Laura,' Daniel stammered; he could feel his face going red but could do nothing about it.

Laura smiled at Daniel's embarrassment and walked slowly towards him and the horse, gliding gracefully like a Persian cat. Standing beside him, she started to pat the horse's mane and then turned to face Daniel, looking directly into his eyes.

'Daniel, I was just watching you. I know you have such great kindness inside your heart and yet you are capable of violence; what sort of man are you?'

'Miss Laura, you read me well. Yes, I can do violence but I assure you that it disgusts me and I'm done with it,' Daniel had recovered his composure and Laura's directness allowed him to speak honestly.

'Then what will you do, Daniel?' Laura was almost pleading.

'I am following your advice from before Miss Laura, me and Ralph will be leaving and you should come with us.' It was Laura's turn to be startled.

'How could I leave my father, Daniel?'

'Miss Laura, you are not only an educated woman but you are blessed with common sense as well. Didn't the cruelty you saw at Blackheath open your eyes? You know what your father's business is about, if we steal and kill we both know there will be a reckoning one day for any of us who touch it, as for leaving you may have no choice.' Daniel didn't realise it but as he said the words both his hands were touching Laura's face.

'Daniel, I have no words to answer you; what are we to do?'

'Just trust me Laura,' Daniel pulled her face to his and kissed her and then they hugged. Laura rested her head on Daniel's chest; she felt safe and stayed there a moment.

'I must go now before someone sees us,' Laura kissed him again and skipped out of the stables back to the house.

Flushed with happiness and a thousand thoughts in his mind, Daniel went back to attend to the bridle on the horse.

'You're playing a dangerous game, Daniel Sibson.' It was Ralph and Daniel was startled again.

'Were you spying on me, Ralph?' Daniel was defensive.

'No, I just nearly walked in on you. Do I need to tell you that women complicate matters?' Ralph walked close to his friend.

'It changes nothing, we're still leaving,' Daniel answered while adjusting the straps of the bridle.

'That better be so, Daniel, cos I'm getting out with or without you or Miss Laura. The carriage is ready, bring the horses out!' Ralph then stomped out of the stables.

Chapter Five
The Tide Turns

The atmosphere was tense at the smuggler's depot in town. Dobson was pacing around the room where Smith, Daniel, Ralph and several others stood in silence trying not to agitate him further. Unable to contain his anger any longer, Dobson picked up a chair and threw it across the room, smashing it into pieces against a wall and causing everyone to jump. Dobson, apoplectic with anger, went to punch the same wall but his minder Harrison did something rarely seen, he grabbed Dobson from behind and dragged him back into the centre of the room.

'No, boss,' he urged Dobson and then let go of him.

'Where is Watson? I want him here now!' Dobson was still incandescent with anger and turned on Smith, who was scared his boss would take his anger out on him.

'I don't know, boss. He was last seen in the Sailor's the night before you left for London, but no sign of him since. We went to his cottage; it's empty of his stuff. It's not just him; there's no sign of his wife and child either.'

Dobson breathed in and surveyed the room they were standing in especially the floorboards that had been pulled up where he had hidden a small wooden box full of money.

'Twenty guineas lost! I will cut him into pieces when I find him; he was the only one who knew where that box was hidden,' Dobson thought aloud.

'Smith, get some of the boys together and go looking for him. I don't care if he's in Brighton, bring him back here so I can sort him myself.'

Smith was only too relieved to have a job to do and get out of the room. 'Yes, boss, I'll do it now.' He nodded at two others in the room who were equally content to leave with him.

'The rest of you get back to work and make some money for me,' Dobson hissed, wanting to be alone with his anger.

Back outside in the alley stacking crates Ralph kept a close eye on Daniel as they worked. Since they got back from Blackheath Daniel had been subject to mood swings. These moods went from being content and happy to becoming sullen and withdrawn. After the outburst from Dobson on Watson's disappearance Daniel had gone into an instant depression, it was written all over his face. After several hours of back breaking work loading barrels onto carts and moving crates around the building the two friends sat outside the building to eat their lunch of bread and cheese.

'Are you going to talk, Daniel, or do I need to start teasing things out of you?' Ralph asked in between chewing mouthfuls of bread.

Daniel waited for a moment, then sighed. 'I saw Captain Munro.' He turned to look at this friend.

Ralph almost choked on the bread he was eating. 'Munro! How, where?'

'In the Sailor's Tavern about a month ago, he said he was there on business.'

'What does that mean, Daniel?' From Daniel's expression and his own concerns, Ralph knew the answer to his question but wanted to hear it from his friend.

'What it means, Ralph, is that he knows what we're about these days and he's one of the people who are going to stop us and Dobson for that matter.'

'Why in the name of God didn't you tell me, Daniel?' Ralph was incredulous in his reaction.

'I couldn't, Ralph. If I'd told Dobson, he'd have slit our throats, thinking us traitors. We didn't have enough money to leave then and, to be honest, I froze; I didn't know what to do.'

'Use your brain, Daniel! Put the pieces of this puzzle together, dammit! You meet Munro here, then, a few weeks later, while we're in London, Watson disappears with his family and the loot from in there.' Ralph pointed inside to the building.

'You're right, Ralph, this Watson thing has got Munro's hand written all over it. Remember Spain? How many times was he sent off by Wellington for a few weeks and would come back with no word of where he'd been? Then, next thing...'

Ralph finished the sentence for Daniel. '...The whole army would be on the move.'

They both knew what was to happen and sat for a few minutes before Daniel broke the silence.

'This is it, then, classic Munro; gathers the intelligence, goes back and plans, then he hits the enemy with an iron fist. We need to get out now; I don't want to be here when it happens.'

'I heard this before, Daniel and we're still here. You better get over to Battle, make your goodbyes to Laura and then we're gone.'

'So be it, but first we have to finish loading these carts then we can make plans,' Daniel stood up and motioned for Ralph to join him. Their morning's work done, the two men and the other workers stood watching as a small wagon train of five horse and carts laden with tobacco, silks and wool was ready to leave the depot for a meeting with buyers in Tonbridge about thirty miles away. Each wagon carried a driver and as security one of Dobson's thugs armed with a musket and other assorted weapons.

Dobson came outside as he always did and had a final talk with the ganger in charge of the train, a Hastings local called Wilson. Each member of Dobson's gang was different in their own way and for Wilson it was his appearance, he wore a brown woollen Tam O Shanter fisherman's beret and had been doing so for years. Although the conversation with Wilson couldn't be overheard, it was obvious that Dobson was still anxious; he was very animated as he talked, as if telling Wilson he expected no foul ups on this run. Wilson listened carefully, then sat back up, tapped the horses with the reins and off the train went pulling away from the depot and into the main street. As they watched the carts pull away, Daniel was unaware that Ralph's eyes were burning into the side of his head. For Ralph, any element of trust or loyalty he once had in his friend was irretrievably broken.

Before long, the carts wound their way out of Hastings and found the London road that would take them to their meeting. Wilson enjoyed these journeys to Tonbridge; he relaxed and allowed his mind to wander, this was always his job and Dobson trusted him, he'd done this journey how many times and never had a problem, he couldn't understand why the boss would be so worried. There were always people travelling on the London road, coaches, farmer's carts and quite often riders on single horses going from one village to another. The two men on horses following the rear of the train of horse and carts, at a discreet distance, had no reason to stand out and Wilson paid them no attention.

'The intelligence from your man Watson is accurate, Captain.' Sir John was enjoying the ride and, for that matter, being part of the operation.

'Well, I have encouraged him to help us and this is just the tip, there's more to come, we have another source within Dobson's gang but I'm keeping that one to myself,' Munro answered without taking his eyes off the wagons.

'Well, very good then, when do we take this lot?'

'We follow for the moment, I have two men waiting a few miles up the road at Robertsbridge, they'll take over from us and we'll keep switching. I scouted the location you suggested to me at Lamberhurst, the road dips down at the bottom of the hill; when they slow to a crawl there the dragoons will descend on them.'

'What instructions have you given the Kent Yeomanry; do they know about the massacre on the West Hill?'

'I've done my homework, Sir John. It would appear our smuggler friends have some history with the Kent Yeomanry and have bloodied their noses in the past.'

'How so?' asked Sir John.

'The Colonel in charge told me they tried to stop one of these trains several years ago and had several dragoons shot out of their saddles. They, like us, have a score to settle. They know the full story from the West Hill and will go in hard; whoever is left over will be for you, as the Magistrate, to charge.'

'This is your operation, Captain; I will be at hand until I'm required.'

Noticing a bend in the road ahead, they momentarily lost sight of the last cart as it turned out of view, they spurred their mounts to a trot to keep up the tracking of their quarry.

After four hours on the road, Wilson yawned and stood up from his seat to stretch his legs while still holding the horse's reins. Turning to look back behind him he could see the other laden carts still keeping up the pace with his, everything was going well and the village of Lamberhurst was only a mile up the road, he would stop the train there for a short rest. The village of Lamberhurst was one of the many hamlets that had sprung up over generations in the picturesque Weald countryside of Kent. It was small with few cottages gathered at the bottom of a steep hill built around a stream that ran through the middle of the village. The stream could be crossed by a small wooden bridge that barely had enough width for one horse and cart to get through. The village was surrounded by trees on both sides and provided excellent cover for a squadron of dragoons from the Kent Yeomanry, who had walked their horses across the nearest fields to get to their rendezvous point without alerting the smuggers or the inhabitants of the village. The dragoons had split into two detachments on either side of the stream. The yeomanry were volunteers who had been trained as dragoons, this meant they trained as mounted infantry and were skilled in the use of the cavalry musket, carbine and sabre. A Colonel Stewart commanded the squadron and was keen to engage with the train.

'Gentlemen, my men are at your disposal – just don't make us wait too long.' Stewart looked at Sir John and Munro.

'I want them on the bridge, then we charge and have them trapped from both ends. I have your permission to ride with your dragoons, Colonel?'

'You have indeed, Captain Munro; we'll await your signal. Do we show quarter?' Stewart was edging for an answer that he would prefer.

'My instinct, Colonel, is that they will resist – you will meet force with force until they yield.'

Stewart turned back to face the village, then whispered instructions to his adjutant who sat beside him.

On the other side of the stream, Wilson could see a coach house at the far end of the village, having taken this route before he knew the hostelry well and was looking forward to some ale and food, the local inhabitants milled around the road going about their business, oblivious about what was to happen. The train of carts trundled forward until they started crossing the rickety wooden bridge. Just as Wilson's cart reached the end of the bridge he saw a horseman come out from behind the coach house. It was late in the afternoon and the light was fading, Wilson couldn't make out who the rider was until he got closer and stopped twenty yards from the bridge. Wearing a bright red tunic, a Tarleton helmet and holding a drawn cavalry sabre that he held point up, it was a dragoon.

'You are ordered to halt your wagons and prepare for inspection by the Kent Yeomanry,' the dragoon demanded in a voice loud enough that the occupants of each wagon could hear him.

Wilson and the others instinctively started to look around, not knowing how to react; at the same time, they picked up the muskets lying in the foot well of their seats.

'What do we do?' The thug beside Wilson lifted his musket, the hammer cocked ready to fire.

'Blast him,' Wilson hissed.

As the thug brought the musket butt to his shoulder, the dragoon saw what was coming and turned his mount, riding back towards the coach house. The musket fired and missed the dragoon but that one shot condemned the men on the wagons to death. The first noise the smugglers heard was a bugle being sounded, they had all armed themselves by now and stayed sitting on their seats but the train was now immobile. Then they heard a thundering noise, horses hooves, it was a wall of sound that was exaggerated by the geography of the hills around the village. The local people, hearing the musket shot and the horses, shrieked in fear and confusion and ran to anywhere they thought they could find safety. The smugglers still couldn't see anything but the noise of the hooves was joined by shouting and then they appeared.

Charging dragoons came out from behind the coach house at speed coming directly at Wilson's wagon with drawn sabres. In the brief moment before the dragoons were upon him Wilson leaned out and looked behind him, there were more dragoons coming from the other end of the bridge, his train was completely hemmed in. The thug beside Wilson tried to reload his musket but panicked and dropped the cartridge, he tried to be brave and turned the musket around butt end to use as a club, before he could do so a dragoon flew past and hit him across the chest with a sabre, blood flew out of his body as it thumped backwards into the cart, spraying Wilson's face. More shots rang out from the smugglers' muskets and several dragoons were unhorsed, but by now the whole squadron was upon them. There was no chance to reload their muskets the smugglers tried to defend themselves with their empty weapons from the blows of the dragoon's sabres but it was futile. The sabres hacked repeatedly downwards until they knocked the wood of the muskets aside and hit flesh. There were screams as the smugglers were knocked out of their wagons, some jumped and tried to run away but were easily pursued and chopped down. Wilson ducked a sabre strike and jumped off his wagon, he ran through the melee as fast as his legs would carry him. Unbeknown to him, Munro had seen him and turned his mount to follow, Wilson heard the horse pursuing him and turned around, before he could see anything a sabre hit him with the flat of the blade on the top of his skull knocking him senseless. The fight was over almost as quickly as it begun. Munro turned his mount and charged back to the fight, a dragoon lifted his sabre to make the killing strike on a wounded smuggler standing with his back to a wagon. As the blade came down, it clanged as it met the steel of Munro's sword.

'That's enough, show quarter!' he shouted again and again until he could hear other voices yelling the same words.

Just a few minutes later, Sir John felt no sense of victory or revenge as he looked at the scene on the bridge. The wagons and horses were still in place from where they stopped on the bridge. However, the mutilated bodies of dead smugglers were lying in or around them with pools of blood everywhere, it was a gory exhibition in every way. The dragoons were all over the wagons, pulling back tarpaulin sheets to reveal the cargoes of contraband tobacco, silk and wool. Sir John was joined by Colonel Stewart and Munro.

'So, gentlemen, how did we fare?' Sir John asked.

'I have three men slightly wounded, but they'll recover, and more's to the point, we have six dead smugglers and four as prisoners.' Stewart motioned to four men sitting on the road all wounded and clapped in wrist and leg irons.

Munro and Sir John dismounted and walked over to the prisoners. The fight and their wounds had knocked the stuffing out of them, they were cowed and scared.

'Stand up, all of you!' Sir John shouted; he wanted them to know who was in charge.

They were dragged up to their feet by the dragoon guards standing either side of them. Captain Munro watched them closely waiting for Sir John to announce himself.

'My name is Sir John Rutherford, I am the resident magistrate for Hastings and, as such, it is my duty to inform you that you are charged with the possession and transportation of contraband goods. You are also charged with the assault of officers of His Majesty's Yeomanry and with the murder of officers of His Majesty's Preventative Service. You will be taken from here to be held in custody in Tonbridge Gaol. From there, you'll be transported back to Lewes where you will stand trial. If you have good fortune, you may be imprisoned, but more likely you will be hanged.'

There were gasps from the four men, one of them collapsed onto the ground and began to sob. Wilson had blood all over his face where he had been bashed on the head with Munro's sabre, the other two men still standing were speechless. Wilson took it on his head to speak on their behalf.

'Sir, you've caught us fair and square for the contraband and fighting with the dragoons, but we never did no murder, I swear it,' Wilson pleaded, to the approval of his two fellow prisoners.

'Ten Duty Men were murdered on the West Hill in Hastings by your gang and you will pay for your crimes, by God.' Sir John was working on behalf of Munro and his intelligence gathering operation, the prisoners didn't realise this.

'We were there that night, but it wasn't us that did the killing… but we know who did it right enough, all of their names.'

The smuggler had turned informant and Wilson was doing everything to save his own skin. Still awaiting an answer from Sir John, Wilson noticed a wagon had arrived, it had come from Tonbridge to transport him and the prisoners; they were escorted over to it by the dragoons and loaded on board.

Before it pulled away, Sir John spoke to the prisoners one last time. 'You have the night to think about what the future holds for your souls. I will speak with you in the morning; I expect information to be forthcoming, it may be the only thing that saves you from the gallows.'

With a tap of the horse whip by the driver, the wagon pulled away leaving Sir John and Munro standing on the small bridge.

'Well, Captain, how was my first mission as an intelligence officer? Did I do well?' There was an amused look on Sir John's face as he asked the questions.

'Indeed, Sir John, we'll make an intelligence officer out of you yet. By the morning, they'll be ready to sing.'

'So, Captain, how long do we have before word of today's action gets back to Hastings?'

'By my reckoning, three days at the most, Sir John, so the next part of our operation must commence as soon as possible, I've already dispatched a rider to Townsend.'

'Does Townsend have everything he needs?'

'That he does, Sir John, we've done our bit here, now we let the plan work and leave Townsend to get on with his operation. In the meantime, we question our prisoners and get back to the south coast.'

They mounted their horses and went to rejoin Colonel Stewart and follow the prisoners back to Tonbridge.

The fisherman's church in Hastings stood alone in the fishing village with the cliffs of the east hill towering over it on one side and where the beach met the English Channel on the other. It was a typical cold, windy morning on the East Sussex coast. The waves of the sea were lapping onto the beach dragging the shingle forwards and backwards with such force that locals walking around the village and working on their boats wrapped their coats tight around them, pulling their hats down hard on their heads lest they lose them as the salt from the sea hit their faces. The church was left open for people to come and pray or to just sit in peace. One man sat by himself at the pew nearest the altar, he thought he was praying silently but in fact he was so disturbed that he was mumbling aloud. The vicar, Reverend Higgs, was sitting in his study writing his sermon for the next Sunday. Hearing the noise, he feared someone was in distress and got up out of his seat and went into the main chapel to find the town constable, Tappin, sitting there. Higgs stood directly in front of Tappin, but the constable was in such a state he looked straight through the vicar.

'Mister Tappin, Mister Tappin, whatever is the matter, are you in need of help?' Higgs asked as kindly as he could.

Tappin was shaken out of his words and noticed Higgs standing there; he tried to speak but couldn't find any words.

Higgs walked up to him and placed his hands on his shoulders. 'Tappin, Mister Tappin, calm down, man.'

Tappin was shaken out of his stupor. The vicar brought Tappin into the study and sat him down; he opened a bottle of port and poured some into a glass. After a few sips of the port Tappin was more calm but still distressed, he seemed to focus on Higgs at last.

'I'm done for, Vicar. I cut cards with the devil, now I'm gonna pay for my sins. Please pray to God for me, will you do that?'

'Tappin, what are you saying?'

'First it was the West Hill: I took Dobson's money and those men went to their deaths. Now it's the Duty Men: they know what I've done!'

Higgs sat back and, with a face full of contempt, looked Tappin up and down.

'If what you say is true, Tappin, then you need to pray and may God forgive you. What did you think you were doing?'

'I don't know, Vicar, I really don't know, but now I have to see Dobson! The Duty Men are on to me, you see!' He was babbling again.

Before Higgs could answer, Tappin had stood up and walked out of the room and the church. Higgs stayed for a minute, thinking, and then did what he knew best: he prayed for Tappin.

Tappin walked around to the alley at the back of the depot; taking a deep breath, he knocked at the door. After a moment, the door was opened by Harrison, who, as usual, said nothing and ushered Tappin into a room where Dobson sat at a table with Smith standing behind him.

'Well, look what the cat dragged in! What do you want, Tappin?' Dobson seemed happy and watched Tappin as he took his cap off and held it in both hands in front of his body in a subservient manner.

'I have information for you, Mister Dobson, that maybe of interest.'

'I'm listening, Tappin, get on with it.' Dobson was back to his normal sneering, intimidating self.

'I was talking with the harbour master from Rye, he says they have a ship coming in from France called the *Bon Voisin*. He reckons it will be in port tomorrow and it'll sit there overnight.' Tappin paused, waiting for a reaction from Dobson, but there was nothing; he just sat there, waiting for Tappin to continue.

'Thing is, he says it's rammed to the gill with tobacco, gin and tea.' Tappin smiled enthusiastically, hoping he had pleased his master.

Dobson let him suffer for a moment, then, taking a coin out of his waist coat pocket, threw it at Tappin, who caught it and touched his forelock.

'Not bad, Tappin, now get out.'

Tappin was only too pleased to get out of the room and back in to the alley.

Dobson smiled and looked up at Smith.' 'Well, Watson might have fleeced me for some money but things are looking up already. How funny: the "Bon Voisin" means the "Good Neighbour". Tappin has told me the same thing as that messenger that Tibbs sent us from Dover this morning. Send a call out to the boys, Smith; I want twenty or more of them here tomorrow night.'

With Watson out of the picture, this was an opportunity for Smith to impress Dobson. 'Let me lead this one, boss, I know I can handle it.'

Dobson mused on the suggestion for a moment. 'Yes, why not, Smith, but don't mess up! Harrison, get me a drink; all this excitement is making me thirsty.' He leaned back in the chair and watched Smith march keenly out of the room to begin preparations; he was satisfied and excited about what would happen tomorrow night.

Townsend hated the cold; he pulled his greatcoat tight across his chest and pulled the collar up to warm his neck. Standing in the doorway of a giant fishing hut with Tinsley, they had been watching Tappin all morning. They watched the constable make his way back to the church and go inside.

'What do you think, sir? Message delivered?'

'I'm sure of it. We have Tappin where we need him; as long as Tibbs' man delivered the same message earlier, then we're in. Right, we have some planning to do.'

No longer needing to watch Tappin any further the two men headed back in the direction of the town. Tappin meanwhile had sat down in exactly the same pew when he was seen by Higgs. No longer mumbling, this time he was at peace. Reaching into his pocket Tappin took out a piece of hard cord wrapped in a ball. He looked at it for a moment and reminisced about all those years ago when he was out on the sea as a humble fisherman, he had no fears then, not even of the angry sea. After a moment, he looked at the pulpit that stood high over the pews, wrapping the cord around his hand he walked over to it.

Higgs was still at work in his study writing his sermon and praying when he heard a noise like a loud bump then a screeching sound like wood being scratched. 'What could it be this time?' he thought to himself. Picking up his papers he went to investigate. The screeching noise got louder as he entered the chapel, then Higgs dropped his papers on the floor and put his hands over his mouth.

'No, no, I could have helped him.' He dropped to his knees and prayed.

Hanging from the pulpit, with a piece of fishing cord tied around his neck, was Tappin.

Daniel had finished a full day taking Laura to her various engagements. After leaving the horse and carriage at the depot, he got back to Bill Crisp's a tired man. As he walked through the door into his lodgings there was Ralph who looked like he was packing his belongings.

'What are you doing, Ralph?'

'What does it look like? I'm leaving. I can't wait around while you whisper imbecilities in Laura's ear deciding what to do.'

Ralph talked and kept loading a canvas bag with the few possessions he had having become very practiced in using his right arm to live his daily life.

Then he stopped and turned to face his friend. 'Don't you see, Daniel? It's all coming to a stop.'

For Daniel, these were strange words and he instantly became worried. 'What have you done, Ralph?' he asked, fearing the answer he would get.

'Use your brain, Daniel. I'm getting out of here, this is your chance to do the same.'

'I'm asking you again, Ralph; what have you done?' Daniel knew he was on to something.

'You know, Daniel, I may look drunk when we waste our time drinking in the Sailor's, but, believe me, I see everything... like the time you had your little meeting with Captain Munro!'

Daniel was gobsmacked and took a moment to gather his thoughts. 'So you saw us then?'

'Yes, I did. I'm not stupid, Daniel; do you really think this morning, when you told me about it, was the first I knew Captain Munro was in town? As it happens. I had a conversation with him as well. I may only have the one arm, Daniel, but, believe me, I still have my wits.' Ralph smiled as he threw the words at him.

Daniel grabbed Ralph roughly by his shirt and yanked him close. 'I swear I'll wring your neck, Ralph! Now, for the last time, what have you done?'

If Daniel's actions were meant to scare Ralph, they didn't work as he wasn't scared in the least.

Ralph looked Daniel straight in the eyes. 'It's simple; I'm working with the Captain, and you know something? It's the most worthwhile thing I've done since I left the army.'

Daniel could feel his heart start to pound. 'Do you realise what you've done, Ralph? You have condemned us both to death!' he was shouting.

'No, Daniel, we both condemned ourselves to death when we signed up to work for a bunch of killers. I didn't mind killing the French – do you know why? Because they fought back! But this makes me sick to the stomach. I respected you once, but now you have sold your soul to the Devil and you disgust me!' Ralph spat the words at Daniel. 'My God, man, should I spell it for you? While you were driving Laura around the county, Wilson and his little convoy to Tonbridge were probably getting slaughtered by the dragoons!'

The gravity of Ralph's words hit Daniel hard and he let go of the shirt. His legs felt suddenly weak and he staggered back to sit on his bed.

'Oh yes, every little thing you and your murdering friends are doing is completely and utterly betrayed.' Ralph walked forward and leaned over Daniel who could only sit and shake his head.

Ralph was by no means done. 'Oh yes, Sergeant Major, I've told Captain Munro everything I know and I don't feel bad at all. Ever wondered what happened to your integrity while you rubbed shoulders with those murdering scum? Well, I can tell where it went: here!' With his one hand, Ralph produced a bag obviously full of coins and dropped them in Daniel's lap. 'I haven't spent a penny of the blood money I earned, I don't want it on my hands, but, as you're so keen on it, be my guest.'

Without a further word Ralph picked up his bag and walked out the door. Daniel had never felt so alone in his life; sitting there on the bed, he mulled through many conundrums in his mind. A comrade of many years whose life he had saved and vice versa had abandoned him, the only woman he had ever loved was oblivious to a disaster that would fall on her father and her own head, and, as for himself, he was there in the middle by his own choice and felt powerless to do anything that would change the outcomes ahead.

Laura treasured any moments of time she could spend alone with her father. She was pleased to see that Dobson had arrived home to Battle and was in a particularly good mood. The thought of taking a full cargo from the ship in Rye harbour excited him and he had put his angry thoughts of Watson's disappearance to one side. After eating their dinner they sat together in the living room beside a warm fire that added to a comfortable evening atmosphere. In these rare opportunities on their own they had a set routine where Laura would do work on an embroidery and Dobson would sit in silence and watch his daughter. Quite simply, it relaxed him and he was content to spend these times with little or no conversation. Laura though felt conflicted; she was no one's fool and knew exactly what her father's business was about. The massacre of the

Duty Men on the West Hill was on everyone's lips and, try as she did, she couldn't reconcile in her mind the fact that the man who had provided for her, loved her and given her everything a young woman could want was a cold-blooded murderer.

Laura broke the silence after looking at a small framed picture of a beautiful woman that sat on the mantel piece above the fire. 'Father, do you often think of mother?'

Dobson was almost dozing, but Laura's question had startled him a little. 'Of course, my dear.' He then took a moment to look at the picture as well. 'I miss her every day.' As he answered, the lower lip on the thug quivered slightly; even he had a soft spot, but he soon pulled himself together. 'Why would you ask, my dear?' This was a term of endearment that he always used with Laura.

'It's just that I miss her terribly as well, father, and I'm scared.' She had dropped her embroidery and taken hold of her father's hand.

Dobson's relaxation time with his daughter was over; as much as he loved Laura, he was unused to in-depth conversations with her.

'Why are you talking like this, Laura? Whatever is wrong with you?'

Laura took a deep breath and continued, 'Father, I fear for you – for us – we must do something different and get out now.'

Dobson was turning from concern to anger. 'Get out now and go where and do what? This is all I know! What has got into your mind, child?' Dobson let go of his daughter's hand and started to stamp around the room.

Laura bit her lip and spoke. 'Father, the whole town is talking about what happened to the Duty Men on the West Hill. I fear retribution, father. This was a terrible deed and we will pay for it, of that I'm sure.' As Laura uttered the words, she became more committed to her cause; she couldn't hold in the inner screaming she had experienced any longer.

Dobson's eyes opened wide. 'What would you know about the West Hill? I have given you everything! You talk about your mother... well, let me tell you, she used to be on the beach under the cliffs, with you tied to her back, a baby, and there she'd be, dragging cargo off boats in the middle of the night! That was your mother!' His heart was beating with anger and he was gasping as he spoke.

Laura though had become defiant. 'Smuggling, yes, father, but clubbing other human beings to death? Would she have done that? I think not!'

She had stood up and, without realising it, had squared up to her own father. The last words had cut Dobson to the bone; he raised his hand up ready to strike her and Laura, seeing his hand ready, didn't flinch. Dobson caught himself and lowered his hand – what did he think he was doing?

For a few seconds that felt like hours, they stood silent facing each other until Dobson broke the silence. 'You are my daughter, Laura, and are more precious to me than anything in this world. Feed your orphans, visit your lady friends, but you will never talk to me about this again. These are my last words on this matter.' He then stormed out of the room.

Laura sat down and silently cried, she loved her father so much and she hated to hurt him but she was no longer able to sit in denial with everything he was doing while she benefitted from it.

While Daniel sat alone on his bed in Hastings, so too did Laura sit down thinking, knowing that the life she was used to would change and fearful that she would lose the two men in this world that she loved most.

It took Ralph the best part of forty-five minutes to walk from the town to the far end of the seafront to the Martello Tower at West St Leonards. Sitting down with Captain Munro, the mood was somber as Ralph mulled over an offer that had been made to him.

'Thank you, Captain, but my answer is no; I want nothing more to do with killing, smuggling or anything like it. Besides, uniforms don't look too fine on men with only one arm.'

Ralph laughed and so did Munro.

'A shame, Corporal, the Preventative Service could do with men like you. So where will you go?'

'That I don't know, only away from here. What I ever had here is finished, so thank you for the money and I wish you good luck.' Ralph shook a small purse of coins as he stood up.

Munro having no hand to shake took hold of Ralph's right arm and squeezed it as a farewell. Ralph picked up his bag and was gone.

The following evening, under a full moon and a warm night, Dobson was in better form because he was doing what he knew best, involving himself in mischief. It was after midnight and he'd spent several hours watching the *Bon Voisin*, the very ship that Tappin and Tibbs's messenger had told him about, as it moored in Rye Harbour. Rye was a small town in comparison to Hastings and, though only ten miles distant, it was very different in its geography, architecture and existence. Rye was one of the original "Cinque Ports" created to provide ships and defence as the south east coast had been prone to attack by raiders from France. With the threat from France now gone Rye relied on a small fishing fleet and its historical role as a small trading port. Rye was foreign territory to Dobson and his men so they held back from their prey, keeping watch from the outer wall of the old medieval road that overlooked the harbour and the River Romney that led out to the English Channel. The town itself was quiet and the locals had long since called it a night so the only people around were the Hastings gang. True to his word, Dobson had stepped back and allowed Smith to lead the raiding party that would relieve the ship's hold of its cargo of tobacco, gin and tea. The harbour area was dark apart from a few lanterns on the different ships as they all sat there safely anchored directly next to the cobbled quayside.

Dobson snapped his spyglass shut and gave it to Daniel. 'What do you reckon, soldier boy? Are we good to climb on board?'

Daniel shook his head. 'We have no way of knowing, Mister Dobson, it's too dark to see what's happening on the ship. The only way is to send a scout ahead who can get a closer look.' He gave the spyglass back to Dobson.

Flanking Dobson as ever was Harrison, but Smith was there as well and eager to prove his mettle to the boss.

Smith huffed and puffed at Daniel's reply. 'Spoken like a soldier indeed: can't make a decision himself and shrugs his shoulders looking to those above as usual to lead the way.'

Daniel had grown used to Smith's barbs and kept quiet as he knew the calm on the ship was too good to be true, especially after what he'd learned from the argument with Ralph the day before. Standing behind Smith were more than twenty of Dobson's men armed with an assortment of weapons, muskets, pistols, cutlasses and clubs. It had been a long evening for them already after first meeting at the caves to have Smith distribute their weapons to them and then journeying to Rye in the dark crammed into a several or more horse and carts. They were growing restless and fidgeted with the awkward cartridge boxes and weapons belts they were unused to carrying. As Smith's words were overhead there were nods and grunts of agreement all round.

Dobson enjoyed playing his men off against each other and decided to indulge Smith. 'So, Smith, what do you suggest we do? You are in charge this night,' he said, raising his eyes in a sarcastic manner aimed at Daniel.

'What I say, boss, is that we stop wasting our time; we've got the men here, there's nothing happening on the ship, I say we go down and take our stash.' Smith was at his bullish best, keen and loud but his weakness was an inability to think problems through instead of charging head first into them.

Dobson pretended to think hard and then made his decision. 'Get down there, Smith, and get my contraband. When you bring it back, you and all the boys will be well rewarded.'

Smith didn't need to be told twice: in an instant, he was off down a set of steps from the wall that would take them directly down to the harbour. As Daniel watched Smith lead his men down the steps he put his military mind back on, it was all too easy. In three hours of watching the ship, there wasn't a sign of any watchmen on the *Bon Voisin*, it was like a ghost ship. Within a couple of minutes Smith and his group were at the bottom of the steps and standing on the harbour quayside. Unfamiliar with their weapons and equipment, muskets had scraped against walls whilst swords had jangled with water bottles and cartridge boxes; thugs and cutthroats they may have been, but organised, trained fighters they were not. Their journey down the steps had made enough noise that they could be heard from far away and that would be their undoing.

The *Bon Voisin* was no trading ship. It was a Preventative Service Revenue Cutter that had been sent from Dover at the request of Captain Townsend. To the uneducated eye it appeared in all forms to be a trading sloop, designed for carrying small cargoes not loads of men. Canvas tarpaulins had been pulled over several gun ports to help with the disguise and it was no coincidence that the ship waited in the harbour in almost complete darkness. For the Royal Navy sailors, marines and Duty Men crouched down behind the ships rails on the aft deck, it had been a long difficult wait.

'When they come, will we show them quarter, Captain'? Sergeant Tinsley asked Townsend.

'Let's put it this way: I will offer them the chance to surrender. If they refuse, we show them what it's like when someone fights back.' Townsend winked at Tinsley as he answered the question.

Townsend, after years at sea, had an ability to move around a ship like a ghost. Unseen to the inexperienced eye, Townsend could see everything and, gathered there on the quayside, making no effort to conceal themselves, were around two dozen men who were armed and coming towards the cutter.

Townsend went back to Tinsley and, crouching down, spoke quietly to him. 'They're coming, you can probably hear them. Pass the word to the men: prime muskets and pistols, and ready cutlasses to repel boarders.'

Even before Townsend had finished speaking Tinsley was passing the word down the line.

Still making no effort to conceal their approach, Smith and his men had reached the cutter; using the rope ladders and other climbing features already there, they scaled up the side of the *Bon Voisin* and clambered onto the deck. They started looking round for movement, but there was no one to be seen. Where was the crew?

Still looking from the wall, Dobson felt confident. 'Look, they're on the ship and there's no resistance.' He turned to Harrison. 'Send the carts down now. This'll be an easy night's work, we'll go down the steps.'

Harrison was off to speak to the drivers, and Dobson and Daniel made their way down the steps to the quayside.

Still searching the deck for enemies, Smith and his boarders were nervous and stayed tightly packed together as a group, then they heard a loud bang from the direction of the aft deck. They looked around and saw a lone figure descending the stairs towards them on the main deck. Smith and his men stood rooted to the spot and time stood still as the lone figure came closer into view and they recognised the Blue Tunic and cocked hat of a Royal Navy Officer. He was carrying an unscabbarded sword in his right hand and calmly kept walking until stopping about twenty yards from the smugglers.

'Who the bloody hell are you?' Smith bawled.

The naval officer answered in a voice that was loud but calm. 'I should be asking you the same question, but, in any case, my name is Captain Townsend of His Majesty's Royal Navy and Preventative Service. By boarding this ship as trespassers and armed with the intention of robbing the cargo on board, you are committing an act of piracy. This is your only opportunity to surrender into my custody; lay down your arms and I can promise you fair treatment and trial. What do you answer?'

Smith knew they had walked into a situation and as he listened to Townsend, kept looking around the ship to see where the threat was coming from but still there was nothing, his mind was racing and he was torn between stepping back and charging at the navy officer. It wasn't just Smith; his men were doing the same, looking in every direction, fingering and pointing their weapons around, huddled together like sheep cowering from a stalking wolf. Smith was an individual who lived on bombast and bravado but what little common sense he had told him that they had walked into a trap. Knowing no other way, Smith reacted the only way he knew how: drawing a cutlass, he turned to encourage his men.

'Watch me, boys, I'm going to chop this fop into pieces.' He turned and ran straight at Townsend, to the sound of cheers behind him.

Townsend was skilled with the cutlass and changed his stance, sword at the ready and watched Smith as he ran towards him, cutlass carried high above his head.

Underestimating Townsend, Smith ran at his foe, thinking him an upper-class idiot who couldn't fight – he couldn't have been more wrong. Smith swung his cutlass downwards intending to split Townsend's head in half, but Townsend was too fast, he parried the downward strike with his cutlass, spun the smuggler's sword down and with lightning speed ran him straight through the stomach. Smith looked down in shock at the sword that was driven deep in his gut, then he looked back at Townsend as he pulled the bloody weapon back out. Open mouthed, he dropped to his knees and rolled forward, dead.

The other smugglers were momentarily rooted where they stood, then one of them shouted, 'Have that man!' They charged as one at Townsend.

Townsend calmly shouted, 'Gentlemen!'

Royal Marines in their red tunics appeared from nowhere on the top deck behind him. Time froze as the smugglers charged at Townsend, their eyes diverted by the Brown Bess muskets they saw aimed directly at them, they ran forward in any case and for many heard the last word of their lives as Townsend shouted, 'Fire!'

There were flashes and bangs all around them and instantly men were flung backwards as they were hit by the lead musket balls that flew out of the muskets, blood spat, men tumbled over, their charge had lost complete momentum as those who weren't hit tripped over those who fell in front of them or staggered around holding hands to wounds. They were smugglers, villains, criminal bullies; they weren't used to people fighting back.

Then they heard another shout: 'Charge!'

The marines ran at them, joined by Duty Men and the Ship's Company who bounded onto the main deck from the hiding places up top. Brown Bess muskets with foot long bayonets pointed at them, followed by the Ship's Company and Duty Men armed with cutlasses, the smugglers didn't know what hit them, and they died where they stood.

Dobson, Daniel and Harrison had walked to the *Bon Voisin,* arriving at exactly the same time as the carts and their drivers arrived, expecting to receive the contraband. Instead, they heard shouting, the sound of muskets firing, screaming and the clash of steel as cutlasses clashed.

As Dobson was in the middle of exclaiming, 'What is happening?' there was a loud scream amongst all the others and a body flew backwards over the side of the ship, landing at his feet – it was one of his gang with a cutlass stuck in his belly!

Dobson was in shock and stood still; he couldn't move or think. Then they heard shouts behind them.

'Hold your ground, you are arrested for piracy!'

Turning, they saw the blue jackets of Duty Men running up behind the carts. Some of the drivers stood up on the carts to point their muskets at the Duty Men but they were too late, shouts rang out and they were flung out of their carts onto the ground, dead. Dobson was still frozen and Daniel pulled him.

'Boss, it's a trap we must run now!' Dobson was in a daze as Daniel and Harrison dragged him back to the steps and started to pull him up them as quickly as possible.

There was a shout behind them as they went up: 'You, stop there!' It was two Duty Men, right on their tails.

Before they could shout another word, Harrison hit each man once on the chin, knocking them both out cold and they rolled back down the steps in a tangled mess. Aside from the Cribb fight, Daniel had never seen punches like them and had given up dragging Dobson who was starting to lose his breath.

'Harrison, put the boss over your shoulder, he's lost it!'

Harrison, as ever, just nodded his head and picked up Dobson as instructed. His strength was phenomenal and, within a few seconds, they stood back up top at the outer wall, breathless.

They looked back down to the quayside and Dobson was jabbering, 'My men, they're all gone!'

He wasn't wrong. The fight was over and an area that was once dark was now brightly illuminated with flame torches that appeared and moved everywhere with a smell of burnt gunpowder wafting up towards them. There were the dead bodies of some the drivers on the quayside with Duty Men milling around them, on the ship they could make out bodies lying everywhere and men in uniform walking over them, some in red tunics.

'Marines,' Daniel thought aloud.

Dobson was still babbling, 'We lost everything, the men, the carts.'

Daniel looked at Harrison, who understood what he meant; they both took Dobson, an arm on each side and walked him away.

The next morning, over twenty dead bodies were lined up on the quayside. Just like the Duty Men on the West Hill they had been stripped of everything apart from their shirts and trousers.

Beside them, sitting on the ground clapped in arms, were seven of the gang, all wounded and, for the most part, with their heads between their knees.

Townsend walked up and down the line followed by Sergeant Tinsley stopping where Sir John and Captain Munro sat looking majestic and in command on their mounts.

'A bloody night's work then Townsend, any sign of Dobson?' Sir John said patting his horse on the neck.

'No, Sir John, we lost him but his men came here last night with blood already on their hands and intent on committing piracy, so we paid them back in their own coin, eh, Tinsley?'

Tinsley said nothing, but nodded his head and looked at the defeated foe, thinking it strange how fortunes can reverse so quickly.

'Good work, Townsend. I want the prisoners transported back to Hastings and locked up in the Bourne Gaol. In the meantime, the three of us will meet back at the Martello Tower to talk further; in particular, I want to brief you and Townsend about our action at Tonbridge.' Sir John waited for a moment and turned to Munro. 'I nearly forgot, did you leave our little memento for Dobson in town?'

'Yes, Sir John, all done,' Munro replied.

'Good. Now, will you excuse me one moment? I need to announce us to the people here.'

Sir John Rutherford rode up to one of the Duty Men guarding the prisoners and, after a brief exchange, he trotted his horse over to a waiting crowd of locals. Word had spread around the town of Rye and back to Hastings of what had happened the night before. The town's people had gathered and for the most part they were silent but there were also families of the dead and captured smugglers too and they were wailing, sad and angry at their loss and because they weren't allowed to touch their men.

'These men you see before you were killed and taken into custody while committing an act of piracy, attempting to take a ship for their own foul use and not for the first time! They were stopped by officers and men of his Majesty's Royal Navy and Preventative Service. I know most of you want no part in this criminality but for those of you thinking about it, this is the fate that awaits you, be warned.'

Turning his horse, he rode away with Munro – the plan was working.

It was early the next morning when the three men arrived back in Hastings town exhausted. Daniel and Harrison had cajoled, pulled and carried Dobson over muddy fields through thick gorse and hedges that ripped their clothes and their skin. They had walked the rest of the night back from Rye across the countryside fearing that they would be picked up on the road by the Duty Men or a patrol of dragoons. Over the years fighting in Spain, Daniel had built up a stamina where he could walk and drag equipment for hours, but Harrison impressed him. True to form, Harrison said little and never complained he just got on with the job in hand to get his boss away from the Duty Men. For several miles, Harrison carried Dobson on his back. Any other man would have collapsed with exhaustion, but not Harrison. As they scaled down the path from the East Hill into the town there was a feeling of relief that they would soon be at the depot where they could change their filthy clothes and have some warm food and drink.

'Nearly there, boss,' Daniel encouraged Dobson as he and Harrison frog marched the exhausted man around the alley to the back of the building, but, as they got closer, they saw something on the main door.

The closer they got, it appeared like a lump of brown woolen material. Then they recognized it for what it was.

Dobson started shouting at the top of his voice, 'You blackguards, how dare you, how dare you? What have you done to my wagons? I will have my revenge!' The man was so angry that he was spitting and jumping on the spot.

It was no lump of wool nailed to the door, it was a Tam O Shanter beret covered in dried blood.

Chapter Six
The Battle of the Caves

The Reverend Higgs was a good man. Compared to his parishioners his upbringing and life had been privileged. Many in his position would have chosen a parish that was affluent and not blighted by the effects of the long war with Napoleon, but not Higgs. As a young man, when he found God, Higgs realised that if he was to dedicate his life to his faith then it had to be more than saying prayers, he would help people and so he lived for the people of Hastings. When they hurt, so too did he feel their pain and this day he knew they needed his words and counsel. Closing his eyes, Higgs mouthed a silent prayer and then picked up his sermon notes.

Coming out of the study, he took a deep breath and walked into the main church, conscious that many eyes were fixed on him. Higgs made his way up the steps to the top of the pulpit; placing his papers down he waited until he was sure the time was right in his own mind to begin speaking. The people of Hastings were religious and that was no surprise. They lived a hard life and all they had was earned as a fishing community from their labours on the sea. Many a fishing boat had gone down in the stormy waters of the English Channel, sometimes within view of their families, watching in horror from the shingle beach. Sudden and violent death was not an uncommon companion in their lives, but this was different.

Like any other Sunday, the Fisherman's Church in Hastings town was packed with townsfolk, every pew was taken and there was standing room only as people crowded into the aisles. Word had soon spread about the violent actions at Lamberhurst and Rye and the people were scared and anxious. Some in the church were in mourning, having had their men killed fighting the dragoons and Duty Men. For others, they had husbands, sons and brothers locked in chains in the Bourne Gaol in town. It wasn't just the families, the community was close-knit, everyone knew each other, their lives, their deeds, their sins, everything. For a deeply religious people there was a feeling that the massacre on the West Hill was coming back to haunt them and that those involved would pay for their sins. People prayed for forgiveness and those who were blameless prayed in hope. Hope that the violence would end, hope that life would be about fishing, living and family and nothing else, they waited in hopeful anticipation for Mister Higgs to begin.

'Dear friends, as ever it pleases me to see you all here in God's house, some of you are here to mourn and I mourn with you.' He waited for a moment, looked down at his notes and then lifted his head, but his face had changed from a somber to an almost angry look.

'What saddens me even more is that there are a number of people here today who have engaged in violence and, dare I say it, even murder?'

There were murmurings in the congregation; people looked down, around, in all directions.

'I am your vicar, not your judge; whoever you are, whatever you have done, my time is yours and this church is never closed for you to find comfort in your souls, but I have a question for you.' He had their full attention.

'How much death must we have in our town? I know you all, you are my flock, my children, was it not enough to lose your menfolk in the Great War fighting Napoleon? There has been too much death of late; we must find it in ourselves to ask God why? What can we do to end this madness? We must all look inside our own souls and seek God's wisdom; were we in our own way responsible? Even in this house of God, a man so persecuted in his soul took his own life. I respect you all for your resilience in the challenges of life that you face every day and so let me speak plainly. You all know right from wrong and taking money to engage in violence and criminality will end in the same way that our brethren have already suffered, step back and resist temptation, what may be an advantage this day will be a loss in the future. I have preached enough; now let us join together in the Lord's Prayer.'

The people of Hastings had listened intently to Reverend Higgs and his words had taken effect. So, as they said the "Our Father", they prayed with an enthusiasm they hadn't had for a long time because Higgs was right, they'd had enough of violence and death and they feared that retribution would not distinguish between the guilty and the innocent. However, despite how ardently they prayed there was a presence in the air that they all sensed, the killing was unfinished and more sadness was yet to come.

After the debacle at Rye and the subsequent flight, Daniel and Harrison delivered Dobson back to the house in Battle. Laura was horrified when she saw the state of her father. The once strutting leader of the Hastings smuggling gang was a shivering, babbling wreck as he was led into the house and taken up to his bed by his daughter. For several days, Dobson had remained in his bed nursed by Laura until he regained his strength and composure. Feeling stronger he sat in his bed drinking tea lovingly prepared by his daughter; Dobson began to think about his situation. Losing men and his contraband was bad enough but his real problem was having no leaders. Watson had disappeared, Smith was dead and maybe so was Wilson. Harrison was a good man but he was a soldier not a leader, there was only one man left that could step up. Calling downstairs his daughter appeared in the room.

'Yes, father.'

'Is Sibson here, Laura?'

'He is, father, downstairs,' Laura answered. She could see that familiar spark of confidence returning to her father's eyes.

'Good, then get him up here, I have need of him,' Laura nodded and went off to get Daniel. Going downstairs she found Daniel sitting by the fireplace in Dobson's comfortable armchair, staring blankly at the fire until his eyes caught sight of a portrait of a beautiful woman in a small frame. Daniel could see the resemblance straight away and admired the image more; the beauty of the woman's features gave his mind a moments respite from the heaviness he felt in his heart. Ralph was gone and once again he was in a world where fear, pain and death were all around him and he felt trapped in it.

Laura woke him from his daydreaming. 'My mother.'

As Daniel turned to look at Laura, he had the bizarre sensation that the image had come to life and smiled. 'I thought as much. Are you all right?'

'I'm not sure, Daniel. My father wants to see you, I think he has plans for you. You'd better go up.'

Now back in reality, Daniel sighed, got up from the armchair and went off to see his boss. As he walked past Laura she grabbed his hand and pressed it tight, she was afraid. Daniel knocked on the door of the bedroom and walked inside, Dobson was sitting up and ready to talk.

'You wanted to see me, boss?' Daniel asked.

'I did, Sibson, listen hard and good. We need to get our operation up and moving again. There's no Smith or Watson or the others, you need to do their jobs for me.'

As always, Dobson wasn't asking he was telling Daniel what he expected to happen. Daniel shook his head, looking down at the floor; he had seen enough death and wanted no more part in it.

'I don't want this, I don't want this any more; I'm the wrong man for this, you need someone else.' He looked straight at Dobson.

'What are you talking about? There's nobody else and don't think you can walk away from me, Sibson. I say when you're finished, not you.'

Losing his temper, Dobson jumped out of the bed to front up to Daniel but was surprised. Before he could stand up properly Daniel had anticipated Dobson and pushed him hard on the chest sending him flying back onto the bed. Dobson was aghast and tried to get up but Daniel grabbed his shoulders and pushed him hard down on the mattress leaning over him, the younger man was too strong for the old gang leader who was now out of breath and lost for words.

'Now you listen here, and you listen well for a change, Mister Dobson; the only reason I haven't split your skull open right now is because of your daughter. Enough, you don't tell me what to do any more! All your best men are gone, so I'll help you this one last time and then I'm gone and your daughter will be coming with me!'

Daniel let go of Dobson and stood back from the bed. Dobson sat up again and took a moment to rearrange himself, he couldn't remember the last time anyone had bested him and he didn't like it but at the same time there was nothing he could do about it.

'Well, well, you have got ambitious, Sibson. You want my daughter, do you? That won't happen, but I'll deal with you a different way. You saw what happened at Rye, we need to lay low and move our stuff from the caves and close down the depot until things calm down. You'll help me do this and, in return, I promise to let you live.' Dobson smiled in his usual intimidating manner, thinking he was back in charge again.

'First, if you think things will calm down, you're a bigger fool than I first thought. Do you think Rye happened by chance? Tappin hung himself in the Fisherman's Church the same day he came to see you! Second, death threats don't work with me; I've been living with death for too many years now, so get to the point!'

Dobson sniffed, having been rebuffed for a second time, but knew that he was going to have to deal with Daniel on his own terms now to get things done.

'Then we were set up, by God! So be it! Sibson, get into town and get as many of the boys together as you can, tell them I've got work coming for them. I'll be back up in a day or so;

when I'm ready, we'll move everything out of the caves before the revenue comes for it.'

Dobson talked as if the humiliation of a few moments before had never happened.

'That's a lot of crates; where will we move it to?' Daniel asked.

'I have my mind on a few places that you don't need to know about, you just gather what's left of my men and tell them I'm right as ever.'

Daniel nodded and went to walk out.

'Remember one thing, Sibson; when this is done, I'll slit your throat myself,' Dobson growled with the usual menace back in his voice and eyes.

Daniel smiled and shook his head; Dobson didn't scare him any more and so he simply walked downstairs. Laura had been waiting patiently for Daniel, when he came back into the living room she hurriedly walked up to him and they embraced.

'What did he want, Daniel? What is to happen?' She looked into his eyes.

'More madness Laura, even after Rye he won't give up. We have one more thing to do with him and I fear it will end badly again. It doesn't matter; after it's done, I'm taking you away, Laura.' Daniel was calm and stroked Laura's hair as he spoke to her.

Laura didn't flinch nor was she surprised by his words but put her head on his chest, a place where she always felt safe.

'Yes, Daniel, take me away.' She hugged him tightly as a tear rolled down her cheek.

Crowhurst was a small village in comparison to Hastings. In 1066, William the Conqueror's army had slaughtered the Saxon inhabitants and razed the village to the ground as a way of enticing King Harold Godwin's English army into battle – the tactic had worked! Over the centuries, a new village and life had grown back up out of the ashes and it had thrived in its own way. Set back several miles from the sea and surrounded by green fields and woodland, Crowhurst was a peaceful place that attracted only those people who lived there or nearby. A perfect location from where Sir John Rutherford could plan his operations without fear of compromise. Sir John looked out the window of his study onto the grounds of the family estate where he had been born and raised. He thought how much he loved his home, his estate, the crops that grew on it, even the animals that grazed on the never-ending fields that went on as far as the eye could see.

But Sir John wasn't looking at the activity of a large country estate; instead it resembled a military barracks. Two lines of yeomanry and dragoons, standing opposite each other, were practicing their sword drills.

A sergeant major, no doubt another veteran of the great war, was shouting numbers. 'Cut one, cut two, cut three!'

As he roared each number, so the dragoons swung their sabres in unison, making cuts to different parts of the head of their imaginary foe, a traditional and trusted practice that the British cavalry had been doing for over fifty years. Away from the dragoons were Duty Men and Royal Marines who stood out resplendent in red woollen tunics, firing their Brown Bess muskets in volleys at bales of hay. Sir John was saddened to see men preparing for battle at his family home but he reasoned to himself that his plan was almost accomplished and things would soon return to normality.

'Well, Sir John, what is our next move?' Captain Munro asked.

He and Captain Townsend were sitting at a table and had been good-naturedly waiting for the magistrate to rejoin them.

Sir John turned back from the window. 'Your pardon, gentlemen, my mind wandered looking at our men outside.' He rejoined the two officers and took a moment to gather his thoughts. 'We have enough evidence to arrest Dobson as it is, but I want more than that,' he said.

Munro and Townsend looked at each with raised eyebrows then waited for Sir John to develop his thoughts further.

'Dobson got away at Rye, if we'd hooked him then, this would have been over but while he can lead his gang this problem will never go away.'

'As you say then Sir John, just arrest him and have done with it,' Townsend suggested with a nod of agreement from Munro.

'No! I want him caught in the act in front of his acolytes. I want them to see their leader taken into our custody. I want them to tell their families, everyone who lives in the town, that the rule of law is all powerful in Hastings, not the regime of a gang of thugs.' Sir John looked at both men, his eyes determined.

'Well, as you wish, we await your orders,' Townsend answered.

'I know these people and they won't be able to keep their heads under the parapet for long, we have rattled their cage and they'll move again soon. When they do we'll be there to take them down. Munro, your spies in the town will keep their ears to the ground I want to know at least one day in advance when they intend to shift.' Munro nodded in understanding.

'Townsend, have we recruited enough men?'

'More than enough, Sir John, the Preventative Service have enough of my Royal Navy veterans to shore them up and you can hear one of Munro's landlubber army types shouting outside, even our gentlemen dragoons from battle are taking shape!'

All three men laughed.

'Good, we have enough of our old soldiers on the streets begging, either we use them like this or they turn to crime, what else can they do?'

Munro stiffened slightly at Sir John's comments but decided against mentioning his relationship with Daniel Sibson. Thinking their business was done, Munro and Townsend got up to leave, but sat down when Sir John gestured at them to wait.

'This final confrontation will be what the townsfolk of Hastings remember. Your men must understand that we are not at war with the local populace but are here to close down a dangerous criminal enterprise. Dobson and his men when we deal with them will be afforded every opportunity of quarter, if they choose violence so be it, but enough blood has been spilled already.' He paused for a moment, then continued, 'I want our friend Watson turned loose; dump him in the town somewhere, he can be our messenger of doom.' Sir John waited for a reaction from the two officers.

'I think I understand your rationale, Sir John, but aren't we losing the element of surprise?' Munro asked.

'My thoughts are that, after Rye, there are no surprises left. If Watson can spread some paranoia amongst their ranks and stop more locals going to Dobson, then it's for the general good. Besides, as the proverb goes, "pride comes before the fall", and Dobson is too arrogant to stop whatever he thinks the end will be,' Sir John said.

'You realise you're condemning Watson to death?' Townsend said.

'Perhaps so, but if one death prevents the deaths of many more men then that's a price to be paid in this struggle, Watson was involved in the massacre on the West Hill, one way or the other he will meet his judgement. Ah, I nearly forgot, his wife and child, much as they've enjoyed living on my estate they can return to their home. Thank you, gentlemen.'

Munro and Townsend got up and left Sir John alone in his study to ponder. While he detested Dobson and everything he was about, there was no malice towards the men in Dobson's gang. They did what they did because the king, the government, whoever, had given them nothing else. If there was work and a way to earn a living for their families they would never need to involve themselves in smuggling. It was up to men like Sir John Rutherford who had been born with every possible advantage to use his means and intellect to help the people of Hastings, not persecute them.

He could see nothing, he just felt the binds on his hands and the canvas bag over his head and there was movement. He knew he was sitting in a cart or carriage; it shook as the wheels went over cobbles and he could hear the hooves of the horse shoes as they trotted. There was no speech, he kept asking where he was going but no-one would answer him. Then he felt himself sliding on the bench as the cart came to a sudden stop. He felt hands grabbing him in a rough manner and then he was manhandled off the cart, he felt himself falling. He was petrified but it was a short fall and he landed on his side, slightly winded he sat up.

There were people around him. 'Who is he?' they asked.

'Help me, please, someone.' He was conscious that people were walking up to him, the bag was pulled from his head. The sun was bright and he blinked as his eyesight adjusted to the light and the faces of people looking down on him.

'Where am I?' he asked, trying to focus on one of the faces.

'You're in Hastings town,' one of the faces answered.

'Hastings? Please untie my binds, I need to see Mister Dobson right away,' he pleaded, struggling to free his hands.

'I know you. You're Watson, aren't you?'

At that, some of the people stepped back.

'Yes, I am, damn you, now release me!'

It was a tiny cottage in Hastings town. The two rooms inside were sparsely furnished but homely all the same. The fireplace in the pantry was well stocked with logs and as the fire burned it gave warmth to a home that was a happy one. There were two boys; they couldn't have been much more than five years old. They were both so happy, each child sat on a knee of their father and they laughed hysterically as he lifted his knees up and down in quick succession bouncing them both around. The father was happy too and he laughed with his boys. While they played the woman of the house watched them and how she smiled too. At these moments she was at her most content, when her man was home safe with the children. How she loved her man and the sons they had, she wanted nothing more in life than to be left alone with her family. Then there was a knock at the door and her husband changed, he stopped bouncing the boys and instinctively reached for a wooden cudgel behind the chair. He nodded to his wife and she went to the door. A moment later, she came back with Daniel Sibson.

'What do you want here, Sibson?' Harrison asked.

'I didn't mean to intrude, Harrison, but we have business at the depot to be getting on with,' Daniel said.

'How so? I didn't think the boss would be about much after Rye.'

'The boss will be back up soon, but we have a problem: Watson has turned up.'

Harrison went back to being Harrison and stood up taking his jacket off a peg on the wall, he nodded towards the door and they went to leave together, not before Harrison kissed his two sons on the top of the their heads. Harrison's wife followed them to the front door. Daniel could see she wanted to speak to her man and walked on ahead to the street a few steps.

'Marcus, please come back. I pray to God for you every time you go out with those people; I fear one day you won't return. I thought Rye was the end of it?'

Harrison held her shoulders and kissed her forehead, 'I thought Rye would be the finish too, but what can I do I know nothing else,' Harrison kissed her again and walked after Daniel.

As they walked down the main street of Hastings town past the rows of fishermen's cottages and traders selling wears from the barrows, Daniel's curiosity got the better of him.

'So, Harrison, you were keeping a secret,' Daniel said.

'What secret, Sibson?' Harrison's reply was guarded.

'Two children and a beauty behind your door.'

Before Daniel could say another word, Harrison moved with lightning speed and, grabbing the lapels of Daniel's jacket, pinned him violently against a wall.

'Listen to me, Sibson; what's in my home is my business. Most of all, my family is no one's business but mine.'

Daniel had been taken completely by surprise and tried hard to pull Harrison's hands off his jacket but the man had tremendous strength, Daniel decided on another tactic.

'Stand down, Harrison, I meant nothing bad. Now let go of my jacket!'

Harrison released his grip and stood back, his head lowered. 'My wife, my boys, they're all I have.' He turned away and carried on walking.

Daniel rearranged his jacket and shook his head and followed after Harrison.

In a short while, they were at the depot and found Watson sitting in a back room, wrapped in a blanket and nursing a tankard full of rum. Two of Dobson's men stood by him.

Watson was apprehensive when he saw the two men. He swigged from the tankard to steel himself. 'I've been locked up by those revenue blackguards; they beaten me black and blue. I want to see the boss.'

He wasn't wrong: his face bore the marks and faded bruises of someone who'd been through a brutal examination.

Harrison looked at Daniel and physically stepped back a pace, he ushered the two men out of the room and looking at Daniel again nodded his head towards Watson, it was up to Daniel to ask the questions. Daniel grabbed a chair and sat down close in front of Watson; he leaned in close. 'Believe me, Watson, seeing Dobson would be bad for you right now: he thinks you've run away with his money. He'll kill you as soon as he sets eyes on you.'

'Run away? Money? What are you talking about? I've been locked up since I don't know when – they even threatened my wife and child!' Watson wanted to be believed.

Daniel waited a moment and shook his head. Munro was at again with the same old methods, the Duty Men were closing in for the final kill.

'How did they threaten your family, Watson?' Daniel asked just to confirm his thoughts.

'This one fellow said he'd seen lots of people, women and children, killed fighting Napoleon and wouldn't blink killing mine – what could I do?' Now Daniel knew it was Munro at work for certain.

'You're a fool Watson, do you really think Duty Men would start killing innocent people, as for your wife and child they've been seen in town,' as Daniel said this there was a mix of horror and relief on Watson's face.

'Oh yes, they're fine I've seen them with my own eyes,' Daniel said.

'I want to see them now, where are they?' Watson went to stand up but was pushed firmly back down on the chair by Harrison.

'Here's the thing, Watson; you have no clout left with the boss. Like I said, he'll kill you, no questions asked. This is your chance to leave, tell me what you told the Duty Men and I'll turn you out of here and you can run as far as you can with your family before Dobson finds you.'

Watson's answer was immediate. 'Yes, I'll tell you, just let me see my family.'

'Good, so what did you tell the Duty Men?'

Watson waited for a moment, looking at Daniel and Harrison, then he answered, 'Everything!'

An hour later, Watson was running through the streets of Hastings, hoping to find his wife and child at their cottage and run away. As he ran through the streets in a blind panic, he felt that all eyes were watching him. He wasn't wrong, Munro's informants were everywhere.

Back at the depot, Daniel and Harrison sat and mulled over their interrogation of Watson.

'Well, Harrison now you've heard it with your own ears; the game is up, Rye was just a start,' Daniel said.

'Meaning what?' Harrison asked.

'Meaning the Duty Men are all over us. If you've got any sense, do what Watson is doing right now: take your wife and boys and get away,' Daniel said.

'I'm not stupid, Sibson, I know what the Duty Men are about; they're getting ready to smash us, but I'm going nowhere,' Harrison said.

'Why not, Harrison? The next time we move, they'll be on us and we're going to die, either by a musket ball or the hangman's noose.'

'First of all loyalty and the same reasons as the other men we use. The boss picked me up from the streets when I was nothing and I owe him. There's another reason, I hate the law, I hate authority, if they gave you, me, all the people here an honest way to make a living we wouldn't do this. Instead, they give us nothing and I won't submit to them. What of you, why are you still here?' Harrison asked.

'I have my reasons,' Daniel answered.

'Does that reason wear a bonnet and ride in a carriage handing out bread to children?' Harrison's face had one of his rare smiles as he spoke.

'My God, Harrison, I preferred your company when you said nothing, as for now we need to get the men together for this last job.'

'What men? All that's left is tubmen, Smith and the enforcers are either dead or locked up as soon as we move they'll have us.'

'Then we get the men to meet us here in a weeks' time, we don't tell them anything except that. If the Duty Men don't know what we're doing, then we can do this one last time.'

Done talking, they went to get the men outside to send out the muster message.

It took Daniel a couple of hours to travel back to Battle in Laura's carriage. As he looked at the countryside around him he mulled over the best way to tell Dobson about Watson.

A while later standing in front of Dobson in his living room Daniel decided to tell him straight; then stood back to watch the volcano erupt. Dobson could hardly contain himself. If he'd been in the depot, furniture and anything to hand would have been smashed up but he disliked losing his temper in front of Laura. Sitting in his armchair with Laura standing behind him Dobson ground his teeth as his eyes burned red with anger at Daniel.

'Have you gone mad, you let Watson go free?' Dobson hissed at Daniel.

'Yes I did, and with good reason,' answered Daniel.

'Well, Sibson, I'm all ears, go on.' Dobson sat up, leaning forward, still just about in control of his anger.

'The revenue blackguards were sending us a warning. They hurt us at Rye and at Lamberhurst. With Watson in their hands they know our operation inside and out. So much that they don't even need him any more. Setting him loose was their way of telling us to stop now before they finish us off,' Daniel said.

Just for once, Dobson thought for a moment before commenting, turning to look at his daughter and then facing Daniel.

'I don't take threats from no man, most of all from the revenue – I've been fighting them my whole life. We still go ahead with moving our gear,' Dobson said.

Laura felt the need to speak. 'Father, the whole town knows what happened in Rye – will you still have men who want to get involved?'

'Why not, I'll pay them well and besides they have nothing else,' Dobson smiled to himself seeking approval from his daughter. Laura however didn't approve. She loved her father but was repelled by his arrogance, his greed and most of all by his lack of concern for the men he was putting in harm's way. The same disgust was felt by Daniel, he had tried to tell Dobson that this was a chance to end the thing peacefully but as usual the man was concerned only with his own ambition and pride.

'I'll go make the preparations then,' Daniel said nodding at Dobson and Laura and walked out. Laura watched Daniel leave then crouched down in front of her father's chair. Whatever she thought about her father's motives she loved him and she was scared.

'Father, I have the most terrible feeling about what is to come. I urge you to think again! Please, father!' She put her head on his lap and hugged his legs.

Dobson was taken aback by Laura's reaction and stroked her hair; he said nothing, though, because his daughter was right, he was too busy in his mind thinking about moving his contraband from the caves. The feelings of others, even his daughter whom he loved, were of no consequence to him.

The word had gone out around the town that Dobson needed men again for a job. The days passed and, sure enough, local men, who had previously worked as tubmen, came forward to the depot, keen to earn any money they could. The truth of the matter was that Dobson was right in his assertion. For certain he had lost many men but people were desperate for work and they came forward. There were other reasons; many people in Hastings felt left behind by the very people whom they had looked up to throughout their lives. The government, the authorities, the landed gentry had done nothing for them. If those in power knew better then they'd be providing the town with work not persecuting the people who had nothing else and so they came forward. For many, it was due to a pride thing, a way to show defiance to the revenue. Smuggling had been going on in Hastings for years; who were these outsiders that were trying to stop it? There was another side to the argument though; the whole town was scared of Dobson. The man was no Robin Hood type of character. He paid those who worked for him but had no empathy or compassion for his gang or the population of Hastings. Dobson took what he wanted when he wanted and Sir John was just in his assertion. Smuggling may have thrived in Hastings but it did so to the detriment of every other lawful business that survived at the behest of the smuggling gang and keeping their thugs happy. However, people wanting to survive concentrated only on the day in front and within a week over thirty men had presented themselves at the depot. They were tubmen, pure and simple – all of Dobson's hard men were gone. They could carry crates but hardly knew how to carry a musket properly never mind load and fire one but that was of no concern to Dobson, he had men ready and willing to do his work.

The mugs of tea on the table jumped and spilled as Sir John hit it with the palm of his hand in anger. 'Damn that man, damn him! Does he not care whether more blood is spilled?' Sir John exclaimed.

'Obviously not, Sir John. Their depot is all activity; townsmen are coming and going, it's quite clear they have no intention of even laying low, never mind stopping. Furthermore, this is typical of their behaviour before one of their operations,' Munro said.

'How long do we have then, Munro?' Sir John asked.

'I think they'll be ready to go within two days, our men here at the Martello Tower should be stood to and the dragoons should be ready to be called out at a moment's notice, it could be that quick,' Munro answered.

'So be it, Munro. See to it, but I didn't want this. I tried to warn them with Watson, but to no avail, I see,' Sir John said.

'You're not at fault, Sir John; Dobson is a wolf and you tried to feed him vegetables, but he'll always eat meat.' Munro walked out to brief Sergeant Tinsley. Sir John felt he had been thinking too much, so much so that he dreaded the inevitability of the confrontation with Dobson and his gang. Getting up from his chair he decided to join Munro and Tinsley in their preparations, anything to keep his mind positively engaged.

It was the day Daniel had planned for and so far things were working as he had hoped. From the late afternoon onwards men had come in drips and drabs to the depot. After a few words from Daniel they left and walked up to the West Hill on their own, no lamps, no torches were allowed. When the men got to the caves they were met inside by Dobson and Harrison who told them they were to wait there. All the men knew was that some carts were coming and when they did they'd be loading crates and barrels on them. Confident he'd had all his men present themselves at the depot Daniel locked the depot and made the tough walk up the hill. It took Daniel a quarter of an hour to make his way to the caves and from the outside they looked dark and empty. He walked deeper inside where torches had been lit and found Dobson and Harrison waiting with the men. Dobson was at the stage where he stomached

Daniel because he was useful and there was no-one else left; with no greeting, he got straight to the point.

'Is that all the men, Sibson?'

'Yes, it is. What about the carts?'

'We lost our own ones at Rye, so I have them coming from Bexhill.' Being questioned by anyone, most all Daniel, irritated Dobson. 'Besides, that's none of your business. Stick to being a soldier; go and farm muskets out to some of the men in case we get company,' Dobson growled.

Too jaded with everything to answer Dobson back, Daniel did as he was told. 'Has anyone served in the army?' he asked to no reply.

'Who can use a musket?'

A number of hands went up, as Daniel asked the question it brought back memories of his first night on the hill, how had things come to this he thought? Just like that first night on the hill the Charleville muskets and cartridge boxes were handed out to a dozen men and Daniel took them outside the caves to stand guard over the operation and to await the arrival of the carts. In military fashion he fanned the men out but as he watched them follow his orders he prayed there would be no confrontation with Munro and his Duty Men. The men were nervous, not used to such work, and several times Daniel went about telling them to stop nervously fidgeting with their muskets. Now it was a case of waiting and just hoping they could clear the caves of their goods and load up the wagons before the Duty Men were on them.

The drivers of the carts knew the way to Hastings and the caves. Like many others they'd worked for Dobson in the past and had no qualms about doing it either, the man paid well.

Their leader was Crowther, he knew nothing about the nights work except to be at the caves with his carts and that Dobson would tell them where to go once they were loaded up. It was a simple enough job all right, but word of the ambush at Rye had spread far and wide and Crowther was cautious as he led his train around the road at the back of the West Hill. Having spent his whole life driving carts around country roads in complete darkness, Crowther had eyes that adjusted well to the dark and could see where the land above the caves blended in with the horizon – they were close. Crowther felt more content, as did the other drivers and men with him.

The tubmen, now turned enforcers, grew more nervous the longer they waited in the dark. In the distance, they heard a quiet rumbling noise that slowly grew louder to where they recognised the familiar sound of horses' hoofs. To the men that noise meant one thing, dragoons! One man pointed his musket towards where he thought the dragoons were coming from and fired. That was it; every musket was fired, some at the same time, but most one after the other. Daniel was shouting at the top of his voice, but it made no difference.

Within a moment, Dobson and Harrison were outside, holding torches.

'What the hell is going on, Sibson? Why the firing?' Dobson shouted.

'It's the carts, I think the men thought they were the revenue and fired,' Daniel answered.

Too busy to answer Dobson went off followed by the two men and found the carts halted. In the first cart were Crowther and another man laying across the bench both dead bleeding from musket wounds.

Dobson turned to Daniel, his eyes fixed in his most intimidating way. 'You have ruined us with your incompetence, Sibson; the revenue will be on us!'

There was no argument to be had, Dobson was right, the night was a disaster already and Daniel wanted it done with it.

'Shall I get the men away then?' he asked.

'You'll do no such thing, Sibson; you'll get those carts to the caves and your men here are to come inside and help load them,' Dobson said.

'Who's going to stand guard then out here?' Daniel asked.

'All I know, Sibson, is that you've messed things up and we need to move fast now get on with it,' Dobson said, walking away with Harrison.

Daniel stood by the cart looking at the two bloodied bodies, he had stopped having any feelings good or bad, too much death had ruined his soul.

The rider put his head down and rapped the reins on the horse's neck as he rode fast along the seafront. His steed responded and rode well; in the distance he could see the Martello Tower. Riding directly up to the tower he jumped off his mount and banged hard on the wooden door. Within a moment he was on the top floor standing in front of Munro and Townsend gulping for air and trying to steady himself after his exhilarations.

'Catch your breath, man, and take your time,' Townsend said and the rider tried to control his breathing.

'Sir, I was in the town as ordered, then I heard musket fire, first one then many, they're up on the West Hill,' he said.

'Can you be sure what you heard?' Munro asked.

'Sir, I was ten years under Wellington; I know musket fire. I saw the flashes as well and then the flames from torches, they're up there all right,' he answered.

'Good work! Get a fresh mount, I need to you taker a message to Sir John Rutherford at all speed.'

As the rider left, Munro looked at Townsend. Taking a quill he dipped it in ink and began to pen a letter to Sir John. Sealing the letter he looked at Townsend.

'We have them, by God,' he said.

'It would appear so, Captain Munro. Let us ready the men,' Townsend answered as they got up to go about their duty.

Seeing the mud-splattered messenger arrive at his mansion, Sir John knew that this was the moment. Even as he read the letter, he had the sergeant major ready the dragoons.

'Sir John,

The smugglers are at the caves now. I am moving my men onto the rendezvous point as planned. Meet me with the dragoons on the road as soon as they can be deployed.

My compliments

Munro'

The Ridge was a road that had been part of the geography of Hastings for over a thousand years. The Ridge was historically strategic and aptly named. Standing on the high ground above Hastings town it was a direct route from the West Hill past Crowhurst and joined the road to the town of Battle. From the Ridge it was possible to stand and look at the town below and see the beach and sea as far as West St

Leonards. As a man who loved Hastings, Sir John was well aware of the irony of his journey as he rode his horse on the Ridge this night. On this very same road in October of 1066 Duke William of Normandy had marched his army of Normans, Bretons and Frenchmen from their camp and makeshift wooden castle on the West Hill to fight King Harold Godwinson's Saxon Army at Senlac Hill in what was now the town of Battle. This would not be a battle on the same scale as that of Hastings, but a fight it would be. Sir John knew he was dealing with a man who was desperate and had everything to lose; this night would be the end of it one way or the other. Sir John was determined that there would be no exhausting climb up the West Hill as the ill-fated Hardwicke and his men had done. Lessons had been learned from the massacre and so Sir John had come the long way. With him were two carts full of Duty Men and a squadron of Munro's well-trained dragoons from Battle. Riding beside Sir John were Munro and Townsend, they had been through these nights many times before and knew that in the moments before an action the best preparation was their own contemplation. They rode together in silence.

Back at the caves, after the incident with the train, things had calmed down. It was now like any good evening when a ship came in. Everywhere was activity; the carts were outside with drivers. Dobson's men worked without interference. In and out the men came from the caves entrance, rolling barrels, carrying crates and heaving them onto the carts as the drivers waited impatiently, hoping to be away.

More time passed and the operation had been going well. Dobson couldn't have been more pleased, the two dead men were of no consequence to him. The last of the crates were being moved outside the entrance to the caves and on to the carts.

Dobson stood beside Daniel and Harrison, hands on his hips. 'Good, I want the wagons moving now. Give it a month and we can be working again. I know these revenue scum, they'll give up after a while.' Dobson laughed.

Within a moment there was light from torches being lit and then the noise of horses moving and neighing. Time stood still, with Dobson and his men watching in fascination, as dragoons on their stallions appeared under their flame torches and then Duty Men appeared, similarly illuminated.

The dragoons were lined up in impressive form, silent with their cavalry sabres drawn. The Duty Men not holding torches were armed with muskets, loaded, cocked and aimed at the smugglers. There was a tense standoff that felt like an eternity as one side waited for the other to make a move. Then Sir John rode from behind the dragoons to the front, accompanied by two other men; Townsend and Munro were both also on mounts.

'My name is Sir John Rutherford; I am the resident magistrate for Hastings. All of you are charged with the possession and transportation of contraband goods; you are to put down the crates and any arms you may have and will be taken into custody.'

There was more silence and Dobson's men looked at the opposition facing them. The bulk of them weren't up for a fight and wanted to surrender, but not Dobson. Dobson, without realising it, mimicked Sir John and walked out in front of his men to announce himself.

'Sir John Rutherford, we meet at last. Tell me, Your Royal Highness, what are we doing wrong?' Dobson bent forwards, bowing in theatrical style with one hand behind his back. The hand behind Dobson's back pulled a pistol from the belt of his trousers and he cocked the hammer of the pistol as he stood up straight.

'I know who you are Dobson and I'm not here to discuss the law but to enforce it, now what do you answer?' Sir John shouted.

Dobson waited again and looked behind at Daniel and Harrison, who could both see the pistol held behind his back. He then shouted, 'This is my answer!' and drew the pistol to his front, firing as he did so. There was a bang and a flash, and a dragoon flew backwards off his mount, landing in a heap. Dobson was holding the smoking pistol in his hand. That one shot from Dobson would be the death knell to every man in his crew.

The Duty Men aiming their muskets fired immediately and smugglers armed and unarmed and drivers of the carts fell down dead and wounded. Above the musket fire, one word could be heard being shouted several times:

'Charge!'

The dragoons rode into the smugglers, followed by the Duty Men. Some of the tubmen awkwardly fired their muskets off at their enemy and men in uniform fell.

Then a brutal hand to hand fight took place between upwards of seventy men in a form of medieval warfare with swords, clubs and musket butts used to inflict death and injury on each other. Sir John had not wanted this, but the fight was on. He used his horse to knock smugglers over with the intention of disabling them, but the dragoons and Duty Men had been set loose and the blood lust was up. This would be no one-sided fight, however; the men of Hastings reacted in the only way they knew how and that was to fight back. If this was the end of their livelihood, they would go down resisting.

Munro and Townsend were in the middle of the fight while leading their men, a smuggler ran at Munro with some type of homemade pike aimed at his horse, Munro saw the man thrust the pike but he easily parried it and hit the smuggler on the head with his sabre, the smuggler's skull was cleaved open from his head to his neck. Dobson fought like a maniac, a Duty Man made the mistake of thinking he was just another thug, he thrust at Dobson with a cutlass, Dobson knocked the thrust away with his pistol and hit his attacker on the head knocking him out cold.

As for Daniel, he had determined that whatever happened he would not kill. Picking up a musket from a dead smuggler he was using his infantry skills to knock his opponents over and away to defend himself but that was it. The problem was there were too many dragoons and Duty Men and their numbers were telling. He found himself backing against a giant rock wall swinging his musket in an arcing motion trying to hold back two Duty Men who were closing in on him, their cutlasses ready for the kill. He was aware of someone behind them and they both fell to the ground as the figure hit them both across the back with a club, then there was recognition.

'I'm not leaving you here to die, Daniel. Come on, we're off now,' Ralph said.

Daniel nodded in relief at seeing his old friend and being saved by him. As they turned to run away from the melee they saw Harrison. Typical Harrison, he was so strong. Knocking over dragoons and Duty Men one after the other with his bare hands until they crowded him as he punched more of them with ferocious power, then they were on top of him beating him to the ground. Daniel went to run to his aid and then saw the mob of dragoons and Duty Men lift up and fall in either direction. Harrison stood up in the middle of the bodies and stared long and hard at Daniel his arms wrapped around the necks of two Duty Men, the blade of a cavalry sabre was sticking through his chest, he then fell down on his knees and rolled forward dead, still holding the two struggling men under each arm.

'He's gone, Daniel, come on!' Ralph shouted.

'I'm with you,' they pushed their way past the fighting and saw a space outside of the chaos, this was their chance to get away, they ran thinking they had an escape route.

From nowhere a Duty Man appeared directly in front of them his musket in the fire position.

'Ralph!' Daniel shouted.

The words had barely left his mouth when the musket fired, the lead ball hit Ralph in his lower stomach and he tumbled backwards falling flat on his back. Daniel was screaming for his friend who was still alive but bleeding profusely from his stomach. Daniel picked Ralph up and carried him back towards the cave entrance, his mind was working only on saving his friend then he saw Munro. Captain Munro was still in the thick of the fight and hit another smuggler on the top of the head with the flat of his sabre knocking him senseless. Munro was aware of movement to his right, he turned and pointed his cavalry pistol, hammer cocked ready to fire. It was Daniel carrying the almost lifeless body of Ralph, their eyes locked for a brief moment that felt like a lifetime as all the fighting around them carried on. Captain Munro lifted the pistol and turned away, Daniel made good his escape, still holding Ralph he ran back inside the entrance to the caves as fast as his legs would carry him.

Dobson was screaming like a hyena. Several Duty Men had him pinned to the ground; he struggled in vain but couldn't move as a dragoon stood over him, ready to strike down with his sabre,'

'Stand fast there, I want that man taken alive,' Sir John ordered.

The dragoon hit Dobson on the forehead with the guard of the sabre, knocking him out cold.

The battle had been uneven from the start and more smugglers were dying than Duty Men. Some of the smugglers turned and ran back inside the cave entrance hoping to escape the slashing strikes of the dragoon sabres.

Seeing what they were doing, Townsend shouted at his Duty Men, 'Follow those men inside and stop them!'

One smuggler, in desperation, turned back before going into the cave entrance and fired his musket in the general direction of pursuers, the musket ball hit Townsend in the chest lifting him out of his saddle and falling heavily to the ground. Townsend's demise was seen by both Munro and Sir John.

'Munro, end this thing now, I'll see to Townsend,' Sir John dismounted and ran to Townsend.

Those smugglers still outside the caves had dropped their arms and were screaming for mercy.

'Show quarter,' Munro ordered several times and the killing stopped.

Daniel carried Ralph deep into the caves, he could hear voices behind him and shots were still ringing as some of the survivors from the outside made their last stand and tried to escape as Daniel had done. He was exhausted with the weight of Ralph and with grief. Ralph was dying all right, but Daniel wouldn't leave him and further on he carried his friend past the areas that were lit with torches. Dragging a torch off its stand he struggled on until he was sure he was too far inside the warren of tunnels. The voices and noises of violence faded away until it was just him and Ralph, he laid his friend down as gently as possible and sat down beside him. Ralph had bled so much the bottom of his jacket and trousers were drenched in blood. Ralph was brave as ever, and smiled as he looked up at his friend. He lifted his good right hand and Daniel gripped it tightly.

'My God, this is like Waterloo again, me lying hurt and you standing over me.' Daniel went to speak, but Ralph shook his head. 'No, Daniel, I have little time. Reach inside my jacket; there is a purse full of coin. I want you to take it.'

'Ralph, no, I can help you,' Daniel pleaded.

'Please, old friend, I have little need of money where I'm going. Take it and find a new life, do something good, for you are a good man.' He smiled.

'Ralph! Enough! I saved you at Waterloo, I can do it again.' Daniel was lying.

'No, Daniel, you don't understand. I died at Waterloo… we both did, in our hearts, and I'm dying now. Trust me, old friend, I'm at peace and I'll sleep better knowing you have a good life. Now take the purse.'

He pulled Daniel's hand to his jacket and Daniel reached inside and found the purse.

'Forgive my anger with you, Daniel; it was because you are my friend. That's why I came back for you. Now go, save yourself,' he pulled Daniel's hand.

Before Daniel could answer, Ralph's head turned to one side and he died. Daniel couldn't cry, he couldn't think, he just leaned down and embraced his friend then kissed him on the forehead. Poor Ralph, he deserved better Daniel thought but at least now he was at peace.

Outside the caves the battle was finished. Small it may have been but a battle it was. There were too many dead: not just smugglers, but Duty Men and dragoons lay dead and wounded as well.

Sir John and Munro knelt over the dead body of Captain Townsend.

'Well, there you have it; he survived Copenhagen, Aboukir Bay, even Trafalgar, but now he lies dead on the West Hill in Hastings. How does that work?' Munro thought aloud.

'I know, Munro, he was a good man and so was every man who died this night.' He looked around as the exhausted Duty Men and dragoons secured their prisoners and tended the wounded. Sergeant Tinsley had been busy and walked up to both men.

'Well, Sergeant, how did we fare?' Munro asked.

'Six men dead, sir, and eight wounded, two of them seriously. As for our smuggler friends, they won't be fighting again; nineteen dead and sixteen under close arrest, all wounded, and we have the prize, Dobson. They looked at the group of dazed prisoners sitting on the ground chained together with shackles around their hands and ankles and there he was, Dobson, his face covered in blood but through the stains he sat with defiance and anger in his face staring at Sir John and Munro.

Breaking away from Dobson's glare, Munro had more work for Tinsley. 'Sergeant, take some men and search those caves thoroughly. I think we got the ones who ran in them, but I want to be sure.'

'Yes, Captain.' Tinsley went off.

For Munro, he had to know in his own mind what had happened to Daniel and Ralph.

Daniel knew there was only one way out of the caves and that was as far as possible from the main entrance where the Duty Men still were. So he explored deeper down the tunnels with the flames on his torch becoming weaker. Hoping and praying there was another way out he could feel the rocks above his head becoming lower and then so low that he had to crawl on his hands and knees. Then the torch went out and he experienced real fear and stopped moving. He could see nothing and so he stayed still hoping for his eyes to adjust.

There were noises that sounded like rats and, for the first time, Daniel thought, 'Am I die to die in these caves, to be eaten by rats? Is this my end?'

He stayed there in the darkness not knowing what to do next. Daniel then fell asleep without realising, his exhaustion getting the better of him but he had the most horrible dreams. He could see Ralph asking for help, but couldn't help him, while around them were dead people and darkness. There were

Laura and little Maria standing together; they were looking at Daniel in disappointment,

'Why did you leave us, Daniel? You could have helped us. Why?'

The images pulled at his heart he felt himself screaming and then he woke with a start. The nightmare was real, he was still lying on his stomach in the tunnel and the pitch black.

'I will not die here, I will not die here,' he said aloud.

He thought of one thing worth living for, Laura, he started to feel around the ground and touch the rock above his head. Taking hold of the burnt out wooden torch, he used it as a blind man would use a stick, holding it in front he crawled forward waving it to find his way. He scuffed his hands and elbows, the knees of trousers were ripped but on he went. He had no idea of time except that he had to keep going forward. The air was foul inside the confined space but the more Daniel crawled the clearer the air became and the small tunnel widened and lifted to the point where he could stand up again, he turned a corner in to a cavern and then he saw it, light! The cavern was illuminated by natural light and Daniel could see everything. He looked up above the cavern and there was a hole where he could see the sky, this was his way out!

The first part of the climb was undemanding, there were foot and hand holds and the ascent went well. The higher he climbed the space around him became tight. There was only one way to climb, he arched his back against the wall of the tunnel and using his arms and legs he pushed and stepped upwards. Already tired he was in agony, his arms and legs were straining and emptying of blood but he kept going. On he climbed and the hole got closer until it was above his head.

One more effort, he got his arms out through the hole and pulled himself for all he was worth, and then he was out lying on his back exhausted, filthy and bleeding. It was daytime and as Daniel lay there he cared not whether the Duty Men found him or not. The smell of the grass underneath him and the chance to breathe fresh air again was too much relief after the thought of dying in the caves. He did not know nor did he care where was lying, after too much death Daniel wanted to live.

Chapter Seven
The Retribution

The streets of Hastings town were quiet. Doors were kept closed as people were afraid to come outside their homes. They had heard the noise of the fighting on the West Hill and waited anxiously not knowing who were the victors, Dobson's gang or the Duty Men? For those families whose men had joined Dobson just to earn some coin the waiting was unbearable. It was early in the morning just after sunset when Bill Crisp could hear a tapping noise. He was in the back of the shop and very nervous. Like everyone he'd heard the gunshots and fighting coming from the caves during the night. Not knowing what to expect he went to a cupboard and quickly searched for something he hadn't had need of for a long time. Pulling out a wooden box he opened it and within a minute had what he needed. The tapping continued and Bill made his way into the front of the shop. He pulled the rag of a curtain slightly to one side to peer through the window as he held a loaded pistol in his right hand.

'My God,' he said when he saw the man leaning on his shop door from the street. As Bill opened the door Daniel fell through it onto the floor, Bill dragged him inside and slammed the door, shutting it quickly lest anyone see what happened.

Dealing with the dead on the West Hill was becoming a macabre habit. The battlefield, because that's what it was had been brought under order. The dead from both sides had been recovered and were in the process of being loaded into wagons. Munro stood over one body that was still lying on the ground. Sir John noticed he had been paying particular attention to this one dead smuggler whose body had just been dragged out of the caves.

'What's with this one, Munro?' Sir John asked.

'I knew him, Sir John,' Munro replied.

'Knew him?' Sir John was interested.

'He served under me in the peninsular and at Waterloo. I even saw him lose his arm,' Munro said.

'Well, there's a coincidence, indeed. Was he a good man?'

'One of the best, as it happens; it ails my heart to see him lying there,' Munro said.

'I have no doubt, Munro. Best we attend to our work and keep busy, this bunch need to be moved down the hill,' said Sir John looking at Dobson and the survivors of his gang.

They were bruised, bloodied and miserable. Huddled together in a group sitting on the ground their hands and feet were still shackled. Captain Munro had taken Sir John's advice and gave orders to his men. The prisoners were forced to their feet and pushed by the Duty Men until they started to shuffle forwards in a decrepit group joined to each other by their chains. Once, they were cock-a-hoop, walking through the town, knowing that they owned it. Not so now, they were nothing but a group of men being marched to gaol and from there to the gallows. By now the events of the night had circulated around Hastings and the townspeople felt safe enough to come outside and see what was happening for themselves. They gathered in a group where the track from the West Hill met the town and the procession made its way towards them. The prisoners walked slowly flanked by Duty Men on foot and the dragoons on their chargers. Sir John had placed Dobson at the front of the prisoners on purpose; he wanted the townspeople to see him clearly under close arrest. More people came out onto the street to watch, some put their hands over their mouths in anguish seeing their men in chains and trying to get to them, they were pushed back with the butts of the Duty Men's Brown Bess muskets. Some realised their loved ones were not arrested and fell to their knees, realising that they had been killed in the night's action. But this was not the only reaction, Dobson had intimidated and bullied the town for years and there were those who'd had enough.

'Not so tough now, Dobson, this time you'll hang!' one man shouted and then there was a chorus of similar insults and jeering directly aimed at the gang leader.

'Where are your enforcers now, Dobson? All dead, aren't they?' The calls and jeers carried on and grew louder.

Dobson looked around, no longer defiant but taken by surprise. He knew people were scared of him but never understood how much he was hated. The grim parade made its way through the main street until it turned away stopping outside the Bourne Gaol in the centre of the town. The late Tappin's men had already been relieved of their duties at the gaol by Sir John. The guards were all now Duty Men, as the prisoners finished filing through the main gates inside the prison yard they were slammed shut behind them. Dragoons and Duty men stayed on guard outside the gates. The message was obvious: the prisoners were there until their final judgement.

The clothes were filthy and bloody, but burned well on the open fire. Daniel sat on a chair in Bill's back room; he had washed Ralph's blood from his hands and the dirt of the caves from his body. Wearing clean clothes that Bill Crisp had given him from his lodgings, he felt better in body but the mind and soul were in torment. Daniel had told Bill of everything he had been through and now clasped both his hands around a mug of hot tea just like the first time the two men met with poor luckless Ralph. They sat in silence for some minutes when Bill heard the jeers and boos coming from the street outside. Leaving Daniel he went to the front of the shop and looked out the window.

'It's all finished now, Daniel, I've just seen your friends being led down the street in shackles,' Bill said.

'Perhaps I should join them,' Daniel answered, his face still fixed on his burning clothes.

Smack! Bill hit Daniel hard across the face, knocking him off the chair and sending the mug of tea flying. Dazed and sitting on his backside, Daniel looked up at Bill, speechless.

'Time for you to be a sergeant major again, my good friend. Now lift your chin up, there's a whole life ahead of you.' He proffered his hand to Daniel who grabbed it and stood up rubbing his face. Bill wasn't finished and squared up to Daniel. 'You know how things will work from here, Daniel. To the victors, the spoils; Dobson is beaten and there's no coming back. The Duty Men will reorganise, then they'll come knocking on doors. Anyone who's had business with Dobson will be in irons by nightfall.'

'I'm listening again, Bill,' Daniel answered; the belt around the face had woken him out of his depression.

'I have no time for your self-pity; the Duty Men will be knocking on the door here later and I need to get my story right and some things hidden, You need to go upstairs, grab your things and go,' Bill said.

Daniel duly did as he was told and came from his room a couple of minutes later with his few possessions in the same canvas bag he had when he first came to Bill's. Bill reached inside his waistcoat and took out a small bag of coins giving it to Daniel.

'What's this, Bill?' Daniel asked.

'Ralph's rent money. I can't keep it, so take it and make good your escape. Now hurry!' Bill said.

Daniel looked down at the bag of coins and looked back at Bill.

'I have no words, Bill, I can't thank you enough for everything,' Daniel said.

'There's no need, Daniel, just go before they put a rope around your neck!'

Bill and Daniel shook hands firmly and Daniel was off out the front door, a cap pulled low over his head covering his face as much as he could. Bill watched him walk down the street a bit then retired to his back room; he had things to get rid of.

Laura had not slept the whole night, worrying about her father. Normally, he would return home by the late morning after one of his operations, but it was now the late afternoon and she had not seen or heard anything. Then she heard the noise of horses' hooves and the wheels of a carriage – he was back and Daniel was driving him! She ran to the front door and opened it expectantly but froze when she saw who was standing there. Sir John Rutherford was there with several men standing behind him who by their demeanour and clothing looked like clerks, there were also a number of Duty Men.

'Miss Laura, I bid you good morning, but I have not come here to exchange pleasantries...' Sir John paused for one moment. '... but to inform you that your father is in custody at the Bourne Gaol, the men with me here are from His Majesty's Treasury, this house, land and everything in it is now forfeit to a court order, please stand aside while we come in.'

Laura stood to one side as Sir John led the way, followed by his clerks and escorts. Sir John's words were akin to a hammer blow and all Laura could do was sit down on a chair in the hallway. Her father locked up, the house and everything she owned to be taken by the courts, her heart was beating fast and she gasped trying to catch her breath. The treasury agents and Duty Men went about their work with gusto. The treasury agents were meticulous in completing an inventory of everything in the house while the Duty Men picked up each stick of furniture and carried it outside to several waiting horse and carts. Laura watched them without watching them, everything had become a blur for her, tired and confused she had difficulty reconciling herself with what was happening. It took some hours but the house that was once a home had become an empty shell. All the furniture was gone, cutlery and crockery also, the house was cleaned out. She sat holding a copy of the court order in her hands. As the last boxes were taken away Sir John saw the state of Laura and joined her, he was diligent in his purpose but was not a brute.

'Miss Laura, I appreciate you are not complicit in the crimes of your father, for that reason you have until tomorrow afternoon to vacate the property and take your own possessions with you. The treasury officers will return here then to board this house up and formally take possession of it and the land on behalf of the crown. If you wish to visit your father in gaol you had better hurry before he is transferred to Lewes Prison,' Sir John said.

At the mention of the transfer to Lewes, Laura sat up attentively. 'Lewes Prison, why would you be taking him there?' she asked.

'To stand trial and then to be hanged, of course,' Sir John said.

'To be hanged?' Laura looked up at Sir John with her chin quivering.

'You have until tomorrow afternoon, good day to you.' He nodded to a treasury agent who hammered a nail onto the front door holding the court notice. Then Sir John and his men left, leaving Laura sitting alone with all her worst fears realised.

The Bourne Gaol in the middle of Hastings town was named after the street it had stood in for over thirty years. It was never intended to be a prison and existed to hold inmates who had been sentenced for minor offences at the Hastings Court sessions. For those charged with more serious offences it was a holding gaol until they were taken to Lewes to be dealt with. The prisoners from Rye had been held there for over a week and had now been joined by the men taken the night before from the West Hill. A gaol constructed with cells capable of holding five or more prisoners was now crammed to the edges with over twenty men. The conditions for the prisoners were appalling. Bored and living in their own filth they sat on the floor in silence and misery; waiting for the turnkey to bring them water or a bite of food. Laura had made the journey to Hastings from Battle driving her horse and carriage, for there was no one left at the house to carry out her wishes; they'd all gone. It was the early evening by the time she arrived at the gaol; it was a dark, ugly building with steel gates and looked even more grim as the night closed in. Families of the other prisoners were waiting outside the gates and Laura was apprehensive as she nudged her way through them to where two Duty Men stood.

'What do you want?' one of them asked gruffly.

'My name is Miss Laura Dobson and I'm here to visit my father.' Laura spoke as assertively as she could, staring directly at the Duty Man.

'Oh well, Miss Laura Dobson, we were told to expect you, follow me,' he nodded to the other man who pushed the gate open. Laura followed the Duty Man inside the yard, he led her inside the building, as she entered the stink of human filth was repellant and she pinched her nostrils. The Duty Man led her into a small room with a table and two chairs.

'Sit there and wait,' he said, walking out closing the door behind him.

The door of the cell creaked and keys jangled as the turnkey opened it. The prisoners looked up expectantly, but were disappointed.

'Dobson, you have a visitor; come up here,' the man said.

Dobson got up and stepped around the men sitting on the floor. Trying to be cocky in front of the other prisoners he said, 'So where's my visitor?'

The answer was a punch in the stomach and Dobson doubled over, falling to his knees in the open doorway. Several more Duty Men appeared and rained punches and kicks down on him until he was lying prone and crouched, trying to protect himself. Seeing the violence the prisoners pushed back as a group scared, away from the door. One of the Duty Men spread his arms wide to stop the attack and leaned down low over Dobson.

'You don't give the orders anymore, Dobson – get it in your head! Pick him up and take him,' the man ordered the other panting attackers. They pulled Dobson up and dragged him into the room where Laura was waiting. Dobson was thrown into the chair opposite Laura. So much had happened in the last few hours that she didn't know how to react and she sat looking at her father. Dobson's nose was bloodied and he sat up holding his rib cage.

'My God, father, what has happened to you?' she said calmly.

'I just took a beating from those blackguards,' he answered.

'No, father, I don't mean that, the house is gone. The revenue have been there today and taken everything. Here, have a look at court order. They even took the crockery, all I have is the clothes on my back, are you content now?' Laura flung the piece of paper into her father's face.

Dobson sat up, startled. 'The house is gone? But how?'

'Simple, father; you lost it for us, same as you killed the men at Rye and those poor corpses piled high in wagons rotting at the back of the Custom House,' Laura said.

'How was it my fault? I knew no other way, my dear,' Dobson said.

'There's the thing, father. You were given the chance to stop, we could have got away, but you were too busy thinking of your pride,' Laura said.

'I did what I had to, Laura,' Dobson said.

'What a shame! An able man such as you could have done so much good! Instead, you behaved no worse than a hungry animal devouring all you could.' Dobson tried to answer but Laura raised her hand to stop him. 'What's more, I'm disgusted with myself for living a lie off your blood money.' Laura dropped her head down on the table and started to cry.

Dobson lifted her head and leaned across the table to hug her, then they both sat back down.

'They are sending me to Lewes; I will be hanged there, Laura,' Dobson said.

'I know, father.' Laura's anger had subsided after crying and she held her father's hands.

'You must leave Hastings, Laura.' He looked around to make sure no one was listening. 'Where your mother's grave is in the garden, stand to the back of the headstone, walk five paces and dig. I have a stash there – take it and leave.'

'That money is dirty with blood, father, but I will take it and find a use for it that will be good,' Laura said.

'Do with it as you wish. Just find it and... well, try to remember something good about your mother and me.' Just for once, Dobson looked vulnerable.

Laura stood up and hugged her father for the last time. 'I love you, father. Goodbye.' She kissed him on the forehead and ran her hand down his cheek before she walked out. As she left him alone in the room; Dobson the brawler, the smuggler, the killer, sat down as tears formed in his eyes.

It was early in the morning and Laura was physically and emotionally exhausted. Her once delicate hands were swollen and blistered in places. They were caked in dried mud and she washed them in a small basin of water while she looked at the contents of a muddy leather bag. Laura had never seen so much money in her life. It had taken an age to dig the ground in the spot her father had said but sure enough it was there.

'Next time you feel the need to dig a hole, you need only ask; I can do it for you.'

Laura recognised the voice and turned around to see Daniel. She ran into his arms and held him tight, crying with relief. After a moment, she released him. 'I thought you were dead or locked up, Daniel! I'm so happy to see you!' She embraced him again.

'I got away somehow but many didn't like Ralph, he died as did Harrison,' Daniel answered still holding her.

'Don't tell me any more, Daniel; too much death and all is lost. My father is to be hanged and the revenue will be coming for the house and land this very day,' Laura said. She stayed in his arms, it was the safest she'd felt in days.

'I thought as much, that's why I watched you digging away at the grave. I had to be sure the revenue weren't here waiting.'

After a moment, Daniel stepped back and held Laura by her arms. Taking a deep breath, he said, 'There is nothing left for you or me here, Laura; come with me.'

'To where Daniel, what will we do?' Laura asked, hoping that Daniel had an answer for her.

'We do what you once told me; we go to America, a place where we can start a new life and leave all this behind us.'

'With what Daniel, how will we get there?'

'I have enough coin to pay our passage, what happens after is up to us, don't think Laura, don't question, just go and get your things. I'll have the carriage prepared by the time you come down. We'll find our way to Portsmouth and go, just do it now,' Daniel urged her.

She stood there for a moment then ran back inside the house, after a few minutes, she came back outside with the muddy bag and another with her own possessions. Daniel had the carriage ready and she jumped up onto the seat beside him.

'Before we leave, Daniel, I need to deliver this bag to someone we can trust, I promise you it is important for us both.' She lifted the money bag as she spoke and looked into Daniel's eyes without realising how her beauty enchanted him.

'That's fine, we best be on our way,' Daniel smiled to which Laura hugged and kissed him with all her heart. Daniel flicked the reins, as the carriage pulled out of the gates and travelled along the lane, Laura looked back at the house one more time. Their life in England was finished, a new life was about to begin.

It had been over a week since the "the Battle of the Caves", as the locals called the fight on the West Hill. Dobson and the remaining prisoners had been taken from the Bourne Gaol to Lewes and peace had returned to Hastings. No more dragoons riding through the streets or Duty Men going from door-to-door. Fishermen hauled their boats down the shingle and into the sea, braving the dangers of the English Channel as they and generations before them had done for centuries. The deaths had taken a toll on the town and there was sadness but at the same time a feeling of relief. The cost had been heavy for some of the families in the town but for the rest they knew it was all over. There was a saying that came from the "Terror" of the French Revolution – "only the guilty tremble" – and for most of the population of Hastings they were innocent and had nothing to fear. There were no more thugs running the town but the rule of law. However inefficient the law and its guardians may have been, the people preferred it to the rule of criminals and smugglers.

Bill Crisp had ridden the storm after the battle. Despite several searches of his shop by the Duty Men they found nothing to incriminate him, he'd gotten rid of things before they came. After that, the men from the treasury came to quiz him about his finances and involvement with the smugglers. However, Bill was an experienced individual and had prepared well, he stayed calm and found their questioning feeble. He was in the clear and his regular customers had returned, he was happy in his life.

Bill had a routine, every morning before opening the shop he would go to the back yard where he had his storage shed. He would replenish the shop with things from the shed but this morning something was wrong. The lock on the shed door was missing; 'Blackguards,' Bill thought aloud. He picked up a broom and used the handle to push the shed door open; he walked inside slowly in case someone lay in wait. The shed was dark inside and as he stepped in he tripped on a bulky, heavy object landing on his front. He was angry at tripping over and swore loudly; turning around as he got up he saw the object he tripped on was a large leather bag. Bill opened it up and when he saw what was inside, he looked in every direction around him and hurriedly walked back inside the shop. Confident he was alone and secure he examined inside the bag further. It was full of money, bags and bags of coins but there was also a letter with his name on it. As Bill read the letter he smiled and felt some genuine pride in other human beings; there was such a thing as kindness.

It was a fine morning in Lewes as Dobson and five other men were led out into the prison yard, their hands tied behind their backs. In the middle of the yard was a large scaffold that had been built for their execution. The gaolers led the prisoners up the steps onto the scaffold, stopping each man by a noose that hung in front of their faces. As the noose was put around Dobson's neck he looked up at the sun and felt at peace.

He had one thought on his mind; 'My wife, my dear, dear wife, I shall be with you again.'

The lever was pulled and the wooden floor disappeared underneath his feet, Dobson swung from the hangman's gibbet and duly joined his wife. Sir John had watched the hanging with Munro standing with various officials from the judiciary of East Sussex. There was no elation or sense of victory. They had set out to break up the smuggling operation in Hastings and had achieved their aim, nothing more.

'So, I understand the treasury wants us to go after Dobson's erstwhile friend in Dover, Tibbs,' Munro said.

'Indeed, they have their own Preventative Service but we can advise them on our adventures here but perhaps it's time for me to retire,' Sir John said.

'Retire, how so?'

'Our job was to destroy smuggling, not the people of Hastings. That trade is gone, my job now is to find honest work for the people, I'm done with catching smugglers,' Sir John said.

'Well, then I suggest we find a hostelry to have a good lunch and raise a glass to Townsend and the other men who fell,' Munro suggested.

'Townsend would want nothing less. Shall we?'

They left the prison yard together, their last job done.

The orphanage at Bexhill was a flurry of activity. The children got their bread rolls but this time they were also given new clothes and boots. In between mouthfuls of bread they excitedly tried on their new boots. The governess had seen nothing like it and was curious to find out more from Bill about who this mysterious donor was.

Bill had been polite and firm in his discussions with her. 'As I told you before, the person donating the money wishes to remain anonymous and has entrusted me with managing how it is spent here,' Bill said as he walked out of the main hall to the grounds outside.

'So be it, Mister Crisp.' The governess accepted that Bill would not disclose the identity of the donor or hand her the money directly.

'Ah, yes; one more thing.'

'Yes, Mister Crisp?' the governess said.

'I understand a little girl died here some weeks back; her name was Maria, I believe?'

The governess was caught off guard and took a moment to remember. 'Yes, Maria,' she answered attentively.

'My donor is keen that this child has a proper grave. He has instructed me that a headstone must be put up' instruct a stone mason and refer him to me for payment,' Bill said.

'Of course, Mister Crisp, that will be done,' she answered.

'Thank you. I look forward to my next visit and bid you good day.'

Bill got into his carriage and sat down. Before he shook the reins to start the horses, he looked up at the sky. 'Well done, Daniel, Ralph would be very proud of you.'

Author's Note

The inspiration for writing this novel happened after visiting the "Smugglers Caves" tourist attraction in the author's home town of Hastings. The story is a work of historical fiction based on the smuggling that took place in Hastings in the early nineteenth century. It was never intended to be a detailed historical study.

The story is accurate regarding the treatment of Napoleonic veterans. There were thousands of them, just like Daniel and Ralph, who came back to Britain after Napoleon's defeat and could not find work or a decent living. Some of them turned to crime and other anti-social activities. So much so that a piece of legislation called the "Vagrancy Act" of 1824 was passed to deal with them.

The bout between Tom Cribb and Tom Molineaux took place in 1811 in Leicestershire, not at Blackheath as in the story.

The story is set in England in 1817 but has two themes that are relevant to the present day. Where unemployment is prevalent and ordinary people have no opportunity to find work; they will always be at risk of turning to crime as a means to exist. Finally, if politicians send our young people to fight in wars in far-off places, those same politicians have a moral duty to care for them on their return home.